To Roy with Love

BROOKE SINCLAIR

Brooke Sinclair lives on a lake in South Carolina with her husband, two children, a dog, and a rabbit. She worked as a social worker and teacher before turning to writing. Reading is her favorite pastime, along with boating and traveling.

NO HIDING PLACE

Brooke Sinclair

A KISMET™ Romance

METEOR PUBLISHING CORPORATION

Bensalem, Pennsylvania

ONE

"It's too late," the gruff voice of her ex-boss echoed through the telephone. "There's no way I can stop him."

"Don't play games with me, Parker. I know the procedure. One word from you and they'll head right for the next place you've got lined up. I will not, repeat *not*, do it," Corey stated calmly, her lilting voice filled with determination.

"You owe me, Corey Hamilton. And I'm calling in my marker." While the silence grew, Parker mentally calculated his options. Anger did little good with Corey, and she wasn't responding to guilt. He'd have to play on her sense of fairness—or perhaps her need for revenge. If all else failed, there was always her godfather Sean.

He needed Corey, and he needed her now. Twelve hours ago the Israeli ambassador had presented him with the problem of Matt Stone. Parker ran a preliminary check on the American professor, interviewed him, and then sent him up to Cape Cod. The moment Corey flashed into his mind, Parker knew she was a perfect compromise. He would have control of the situation and yet, if it all blew up in his face, he'd have no official responsibility. All Parker had to do was convince Corey.

After pausing long enough to keep her temper in check, Corey continued. "I don't owe you anything. I figure that we're more than even in anyone's book." Letting herself voice a touch of the anger that she was feeling, she asked, "Why in the world would you even think of me? You know that I've been off the active-duty roster for more than a year now, and I don't plan to change my status."

After another lengthy silence, Parker said matter-of-factly, "I need you." When no further comments came, Parker sighed and played his last card. "Do this for me, Corey, and I'll call it quits for good. I'll take you off indefinite leave and officially end your employment. Full retirement."

"No strings?" Running her long fingers through her short blond hair, Corey stood, rubbing one bare foot against her calf, wondering if she could trust Parker. "I'd be out? What's the catch? Just how hot is this guy?"

"I don't know. He's a wild card that the Israelis dumped on me twelve hours ago. He checks out as legit on the surface. I'm about ninety percent certain that your main problem will be keeping the guy *in*, not keeping someone away from him. What's the matter? Don't you think you can control one civilian anymore? A college professor with a broken leg?" When Corey didn't respond, Parker added the one piece of information that made him think of her in the first place, the hook that he hoped would prove to be irresistible. "According to the Israelis, the People's Front is after him."

With a sigh, Corey agreed to listen. She was thinking of her last experience with the PF group. She owed those people. This could be a fitting end to her agency life. "Give me the details."

Smiling, Parker answered briskly. "He's a professor, Political Science at Berkeley. Widower, well respected. The Israelis rescued him in Lebanon, patched him up, and sent him to me. I don't really expect any trouble. If anything comes up, you know the routine. Sit tight and call for help. We all know," Parker said dryly, "that your house is as safe as a fort."

"One month, Parker," the blond woman agreed. "I'll give him one month." Before Parker could thank her, Corey cut in. "On two conditions. You send me my severance papers within twenty-four hours," she stated, pausing for effect. "With Sean included on my full medical policy."

Swallowing his short-lived feeling of success, Parker reluctantly agreed. She was calling in his last hold over her. The only thing that kept Corey from resigning outright was her godfather's expensive nursing home. Neither Corey nor Sean McCaulley himself could afford it without the generous medical policy that the government provided for its agents and their families. "Okay. You're out and Sean's got his insurance."

"You got a deal. I'll take Stone in today, but no papers and he's back with your guys tomorrow by noon." With that, Corey hung up and turned to look at her pale face in the mirror that hung over her thirties-style telephone. The antique glass gave her face a slightly wavy look but couldn't disguise the frown that forced her full lips into a tight grimace. At first glance, dressed as she was in an oversize sweater and tight brown corduroy jeans, she looked more like a teenager than a mature woman of twenty-nine. A closer look at her blue eyes, however, revealed a wariness that only time and experience could produce. Now cautious hope shone through, a hope that she might finally be free.

Wandering out from her small office, Corey checked the nearest clock, a Seth Thomas Regulator that hung in her private quarters, noting that it was only nine A.M. Out of habit, she opened the door that separated her living quarters from her antique shop.

Assured everything was ready, she walked up the narrow, steep stairs that bisected the building, wondering if she'd done the right thing. This wasn't the first time that Parker had tried to tempt her back with an assignment. But it was the first time he had offered her something she couldn't refuse. Freedom for Sean and herself all tied up in a package that promised some justice for the Syrian PF.

Suddenly pleased, Corey grabbed some fresh sheets and moved toward her spare bedroom. It might even be nice, having some company for a change. As long as this professor wasn't expecting much luxury. More important than that, she hoped that he'd be able to maneuver himself up the stairs into his room. Broken leg or not, she wasn't about to carry him.

Leaning forward, Matt Stone pushed aside the curtains on the back door of the paneled van and gazed at the old two-story house beside him. He distinctly remembered Parker telling him that the name of his hiding place was the Antique Emporium. If this was the place, it wasn't what he expected. The store, or house, whatever it was, was old and its gray wooden siding was in dire need of paint. It was separated from its neighboring establishments, all in more or less the same state of semidisrepair, by a small side yard on one side and by the tall dunes on the left. Impulsively, he started to open the van's back door, repressing a groan when he finally straightened out his left leg, only to hear the driver snap an order back at him to stay put until he drove around to the back.

Matthew Stone was not happy. He was tired, filthy, and his leg ached intolerably from the forced inactivity of the last two days. Ever since he'd been rescued, he'd been treated like an object, shuffled from one place to another without any regard to his feelings. Aside from the physical pain, Matt realized that he was reaching the end of his emotional tether. He badly needed a time to rest, to somehow integrate this past month, indeed this past year, into his life.

As soon as Corey heard the low beep that signaled someone's presence on her back porch, she ran down the steps and cautiously opened the back door of the shop. She found herself staring up, way up into a pair of furious eyes, deep blue eyes whose lighter blue specks made them sparkle with anger. At five feet nine, Corey wasn't used to looking up at many people, but she found herself looking up at this man. A lock of wavy black hair fell over his forehead, and he shook his head in a vain attempt to remove the offending curl from his eyes. His startling eyes were set in a strong face, good-looking yet full of character. Golden-brown skin hinted of sunbaked days or, perhaps, Mediterranean ancestry. His mouth was taut with anger, pulling the skin over his high cheekbones and accentuating his firm jaw and square chin. The only feature that deviated from absolute perfection was his nose, which was slightly crooked as though once broken. He was standing beside one suitcase while holding a piece of carry-on luggage in one hand and leaning on a sturdy cane with the other.

"This is the Antique Emporium, isn't it?" he asked in a deep, resonant voice, shifting his weight on his good leg. His eyes looked through her, automatically dismissing her as unimportant. "Where is Hamilton? Didn't he know I was coming?" Frustration colored his voice as he rattled off his questions, leaving no chance for Corey to respond.

She stepped back into her enclosed porch as she motioned the man to enter the back room, pulling his suitcase in behind him as she rapidly closed the door. She stood up, deliberately insolent as she looked him over. He was tall, at least six feet four, and lean. A leather flight jacket accentuated his trim waist and led her eyes down to a pair of jeans that had seen far better days. One pants leg was slit up to the knee and a filthy walking cast protruded from its ragged edges. His jeans fit the other leg to perfection, hugging a well-shaped calf, displaying long, well-developed muscles.

"Who the hell are you?" Matthew Stone demanded irritably, leaning against the side of the small porch, more tired and uncomfortable than he wanted to admit. Now that the danger was supposedly over, he wanted to forget it all and get some rest. "Can you talk, sweetheart, or are you going to stand there just admiring the merchandise?"

Anger kept him going, indignation at the way he'd been left on the back door of this rickety shop, like left luggage or an UPS package. His leg ached in the dampness that passed for a New England spring, his arms were tired, even his eyes stung from lack of sleep. After all he'd been through, he should have expected this. It was only appropriate that Hamilton was nowhere to be seen. "Well, can you at least speak?'' he demanded of Corey. "Where is this Corey Hamilton? Tell him that Parker sent me.''

With a barely noticeable grimace, Corey responded. "Hate to tell you this, Dr. Stone, but I'm Corey Hamilton." Sticking her hand out in greeting, she added, "Everything's nearly ready. Parker didn't tell me you were coming so early. I was led to believe you'd be arriving at noon.''

"I was led to believe that you were a man!" Matt replied with both a hint of anger and a trace of amusement. "Are you the Corey Hamilton who works for Parker and who's supposed to protect me? You look like you're twelve years old and couldn't hold off a troup of Girl Scouts!"

Corey stood unmoved, waiting patiently for him to shake the hand she'd extended. When she held her ground, Matt began to revise his opinion of the woman in front of him. She was tall and slim, her bulky sweater concealing more than it revealed. Her legs were fabulous, though, encased in skintight brown corduroy jeans that were so well worn that the fabric looked powdery and velvet smooth.

Running his eyes over her body in an inspection similar to the one she had given him, he lingered a moment on her long, graceful neck and then moved up to meet sardonic eyes, gazing patiently into his. Her curly blond hair was short, and casually cut, framing her delicate face in a golden halo. At first glance, she looked like the girl next door, but not upon closer inspection. Then her beauty became apparent—in the delicate turn of her nose, the oval-shaped face and perfect bones. When Matt looked fully into her deep blue eyes, he realized Corey Hamilton was no innocent. Her eyes were somber, full of restraint, regret, and an inner strength of spirit.

After several seconds of silent appraisal, during which Corey remained completely impassive, Matt struggled to shift more of his weight on his cane, dropping his suitcase in order to shake her still-outstretched hand. His strong hand enfolded her slender one, and they briefly touched. Corey reached down to grab Stone's carryall, automatically glancing up and down alleys through the side window. "I think it's time we got you off the porch. Come in, and sit down before you fall over."

"You're a woman!"

"Your powers of observation must serve you well in your line of work," Corey noted dryly. Then, exactly matching his condescending tone, she turned to him, an eyebrow raised and asked, "You are a professor?"

With an ironic grin, Matt unbent a trifle, unleashing a charm and charisma that not even Corey could totally ignore. When he smiled, his entire face lit up, turning his somber good looks into something altogether breathtaking. "I deserved that, I guess. Sorry. I expected an older man, not a young girl, when Parker mentioned you. You're connected to the agency?" he inquired, polite disbelief in his voice. "Was your father an agent or," with a slight wave of his hand and a deliberate downturn of his full lips, "you're married to an agent? Is that how you got your clearance?"

Watch it, Corey thought as he spoke. *This man is used to getting everything his way*. His studied smile and deliberately casual gestures were designed to charm. With looks like his, he had to be used to female attention, used to exploiting his obvious attributes to get his own way. Taking a deep breath, Corey forced herself to answer his questions politely. He was going to be rudely surprised if he expected her to fall over him.

"My clearance is my own, Dr. Stone," Corey said over her shoulder, leading him back into her personal quarters.

"Do you live here alone?"

"Until today. Sit down," Corey told the man, pulling a needlepoint footstool over in front of a comfortable wing chair. "You look like you're in pain."

"I'm not exactly ready for a marathon," Matt admitted ruefully. He'd thought he had been concealing his discomfort quite adequately.

"Sit down. I'll fix you a cup of coffee and get you settled. Have you eaten yet?"

"Yes, thank you. We had breakfast of sorts on the road. Coffee sounds wonderful, though," Matt stated as he settled back onto the comfortable chair and gratefully propped up his throbbing leg on the footstool. He was pleasantly surprised to find himself in a modern, comfortable living room.

Gazing around, he took an inventory of the room while he wondered about the woman. Trying to gain a clue to his new keeper's personality, he looked carefully around the room. Antiques were blended with modern comfort, creating a style that pleased the eye and the body. A bookcase was full of a jumbled assortment of hard-cover and paperback books. A large rolltop desk occupied one corner of the room, and, surprisingly, an entire wall was taken up with the most modern and sophisticated of entertainment systems, right down to a CD player. As Matt leaned back, soaking up the normalcy of the room, he began to relax for the first time since he'd landed in the Middle East ten months ago.

Now that the immediate danger had ebbed, Matt felt more like himself. He could deal with this situation all on his own. A month alone with a beautiful woman was just what he needed to take his mind off the past few months. As images of that time flashed through his mind, Matt deliberately banished them. He refused to think of anything right now but the woman who was in the other room. If this lady was a spy, who knew what else she was? Maybe she was lonely, too, and they could spend the next month comforting each other. It was the best idea he'd had in a very long time.

Corey walked into the kitchen and filled the kettle with water. She moved to gather up the cups and instant coffee. Her mind rapidly outlined the trouble that she knew she was going to face for the next month. She had expected a stereotyped professor, white hair and absentminded, pipes and long lectures. What she got was the exact opposite. The man was absolutely, knock-your-socks-off gorgeous. And, from his arrogant greeting, he was well aware of his own charm and not averse to using it to his own advantage. While Corey told herself that it was his arrogance that would be hard to deal with professionally, a small part of her mind said his charm might be able to affect her in a more personal way. Clamping down on her imagination, she forced herself to think of Stone as only a means to an end. It was just another job, her final one for Parker.

Composing her face into a neutral smile, Corey poured the hot water into the heavy mugs, mixing the mocha blend thoroughly. She walked out to find

Stone carefully inspecting her living room. "Does it meet with your high standards, Dr. Stone?"

"It's unique, like its owner," Matt replied, staring at her closely. In the brighter light, he realized she was older than he'd originally estimated, more not less attractive. "Have you lived here long?"

"Let's quit fencing, Dr. Stone, and get this out in the open. We are going to be together for a month, and I'd just as soon lay some ground rules right now."

"Fine with me, Ms. Hamilton, or is it Mrs.? Parker obviously didn't tell me much about you," Matt said slowly, enjoying the slight thinning of her exotic lips. Suddenly some of his fatigue and much of his worry lifted. For a few minutes he let himself revert back to his old self, one lost many years ago in pain and anger. He hadn't flirted with a woman since before he'd married. "I do wonder at your background, since I'll be at your mercy, more or less."

"A perfectly fair question, Dr. Stone."

Before she could continue, Matt broke into the conversation, "Call me Matt, please. Only my students call me Dr. Stone, and I doubt that there's much I can teach you. You'll have to be the instructor while I'm here." Pausing, he deliberately let his voice fall seductively. "Or perhaps we could teach each other all about our respective fields?"

"All right," Corey said evenly, counting to ten mentally as she wondered what he thought she'd done as an agent. If he didn't watch it, he would find out, in a more physical manner than he expected. "No more Doctor. You may call me Corey, or Hamilton, whatever you please."

"All right, Corey. I agree that we need some ground rules, and since it's your ground, why don't you start?"

"Tell me about your book and who's after you."

"Right to the point, huh? Okay," Matt said, suddenly not quite as relaxed as he leaned back and laced his fingers behind his neck. Briefly he wished that she'd let him forget the entire affair for at least one day but knew that reality was her job as well as his. He was no more that carefree professor than she was an innocent antique dealer.

"It's a book about the inner workings of the oil cartel, their secret financial deals with Libya, their relation to the West. An ex-student gave me some inside information that led me to a cartel of oil men who are secretly financing a great deal of the underground terrorist operations, particularly the Syrian PF. My informant gave me some of the financial proof I needed to trace the money trail—before they had him killed. When he was hit by a car, I tried to get away, too. Some Israeli agents saved me, thinking I was another American destined for kidnapping. The Israelis set my leg and, when they found out about my book, they sent me to Parker. He thought I could finish the book up here. I should be perfectly safe once I get my rough draft to my publisher. Does that answer your question?"

Corey wondered for a moment which Arab sheik was doing the financing but decided that details would come later. This was the time for basics. "For now. Does anyone know you're here?"

"Just Parker and the two men who drove me up here."

"Besides them. Did you call anyone—housekeeper, lover, friend—before you came here?"

"When would I get a chance?" Matt asked. "Someone's been with me every minute of every day for the past four weeks. I called my publisher and the dean from Washington, telling them I'd be back in a month. Parker monitored both calls, if you're so interested. Are you asking if I'm available or were you only interested in my security?'' Matt inquired with a small smile.

"Security," Corey explained a trifle sharply as she intentionally allowed a brief flash of temper to surface. "I know the basic facts of your life already, from Parker. I personally don't care if you have an entire harem waiting for you in California, all nude in a hot tub, so long as you don't contact them until you're out of here.''

"For the record, then, there's no one special waiting for me." A momentary look of pain crossed his face as he remembered his murdered wife, but Matt banished it. He was going to take this month as a respite from all of the pain. For once, he was going to enjoy himself with this beautiful woman who was both his captor and his captive.

As that thought crossed his mind, Matt grimaced. It was not in his character to force himself on any reluctant female. Aside from the fact that he had never needed to, he detested men who did. Yet, he felt compelled to tease her, making cracks that he would normally never even think, let alone voice. It had to be a result of the past forty-eight hours, and his state of complete exhaustion. By morning, he'd stop feeling like a seventeen-year-old lusting after his first woman.

"Good, that makes it easier." Setting her empty mug down, Corey addressed the tall man who was watching her with quizzical blue eyes. "My rules are simple. Have you heard of the Indian practice of purdah?'' When Matt nodded his head, she went on. "That's what this is until you're finished with your book. You don't contact anyone. You don't leave the house. You don't let anyone know you are here, anyway. Now, do you want to ask me anything or are you ready to see your room?''

"I want to ask you lots of things, but I'm tired and my leg aches. Do you mind showing me my room and we can continue this conversation later?"

Instantly sympathetic, Corey stood up and hefted Matt's suitcase before he could drag himself upright. "It must have been a long trip, if Parker sent you up here first class."

"First class?" Matt exclaimed. "Riding in the back of one truck, being ferried to New York by helicopter and then shoved in the back of a van for five hours is not what I call traveling first class," Matt noted. "Although the accommodations are definitely in a category by themself. Do all safe houses come with beautiful women or only the ones for the men?''

Glaring at him over her shoulder, Corey marched up the stairs less slowly than she normally would have, brusquely telling him to follow her. After a few steps, Corey stopped and turned. "Don't think that this is not serious because I'm a woman, or that this is not a dangerous situation. Sex has nothing to do with this. You're here because I—''

Stopping her explanation, Corey looked him directly in the eye. "Damn it, Stone. This is official business and nothing more. I can understand how hard this must be, how helpless you must feel, but if Parker was that careful with you, you are in real danger. This is no game. You were free or they wouldn't have dropped you here, but I still haven't gotten the final all clear. From now on," Corey told him, staring directly into his eyes, "you don't do anything, any one little thing," she said, deliberately poking his chest with one stiff finger to illustrate her point, "without my permission!" Turning quickly, she walked rapidly up the rest of the steps.

Walking to the first door on the right, Corey moved swiftly into the room and opened the window curtains. This room was normally hers, but she thought that a man Matt's size deserved the only double bed in the house. Besides, it was the least accessible room in the house. She quickly gazed over the quilted bedspread and was grateful that she'd changed the sheets just last night.

The bed was a Cannonball style with four huge posters rising toward the ceiling, looking for all the world as if they deserved a canopy to cover them. Corey efficiently deposited Matt's scuffed leather suitcase down on the low dresser, sweeping her cosmetics into a top drawer.

"Is this your room?" Matt murmured in surprise, looking puzzled. Books sat on the table beside the bed, and a small color TV rested on top of a lovely campaign chest against the far wall. The room was done in varying shades of gold and browns. It should have looked masculine, given the color scheme, but it didn't. It merely looked warm and comforting.

"It's the only double bed. I'll sleep in the guest room."

"We could always share?" Matt suggested, unable to resist one more crack. Chagrined, he admitted to himself that she did have a point. This macho reaction came in part from a need to gain some power in this situation. At least, part of it. The other part was that he was honestly attracted to this woman, instantly and completely sure that they could be good for each other.

"The only thing we're going to share," she told him seriously, "is the bathroom. And not at the same time. It's the next door down the hall. I'll be back later to move my stuff out of here. You lie down and I'll go see if you can stay."

"What do you mean if I can stay? Of course I'm staying."

"Not until I get the final all clear from Parker. Look . . ." Corey said in a softer tone, her heart reacting unwillingly to the hint of pain shadowing those intense blue eyes. "You take a couple of aspirin and lie down. There's some in the bathroom cabinet. It'll probably be fine. I'll call you for lunch."

TWO

Corey walked to the front of her shop two hours later and stood with her forehead pressed against the glass, gazing out to the street. Matt could stay. She wondered why she felt so relieved. Matt had passed Parker's second security check with flying colors. The men who'd delivered Stone guaranteed they hadn't been followed. All was clear.

Why did she care? She would be free of Parker if Matt stayed. That was the one and only reason it mattered. It had to be. Even if Matt was attractive, and even if he kept making passes, Corey knew she couldn't respond. She would never again mix business with pleasure. Stone was nothing more than her last assignment. Nothing more. Turning into the kitchen to start lunch, she feared she'd have to keep reminding herself of that, over and over again.

Minutes later, carrying the tray with Matt's lunch, she tapped gently on her own bedroom door. When he didn't respond, Corey slowly edged the door open. She was unable to resist staring at the man asleep so carelessly on her bed. He'd taken off his shoes and his jacket in a concession to comfort but was otherwise fully dressed. And sexy as any man could ever be.

21

Corey set the tray down and walked softly over to the bed. She couldn't help but notice his long lashes, spread like a fan across his tanned cheeks, the thick black lines of his brows and the way his hair fell so boyishly across his smooth brow. When she reached out to touch his shoulder, her hand was captured and pulled down toward his chest. Reflexes took over. Corey went with the flow of his movement, and as he pulled, she twisted his arm, abruptly shifting his weight against his own body. Seconds later he lay flat on his stomach, with his arm pulled up to the middle of his back, Corey leaning over him in control.

It was a toss-up as to whom was the most surprised. After a second, Corey released his arm and apologized. "Sorry, I didn't mean to do that. You surprised me. Did I hurt you?"

Matt rolled over and looked up into her lovely blue eyes, stunned at her speed and agility. "Well, lady. You just convinced me. I guess you really are legitimate. How did you do that?"

"Leverage and reflexes, that's all. How's your leg?"

"Fine. I didn't hit anything with it. The only thing that's damaged is my pride. I've never had a woman do anything like that to me in bed before."

"There's a first time for everything," Corey retorted before deliberately changing the subject. She had no intention of letting Matt goad her into discussing anything remotely sexual. "Are you ready for lunch?"

When Matt nodded, she carried his tray over to the bedtable. "I thought you might want to take your meals up here, considering your cast."

"Back up a minute. What happened? Am I staying?"

"Yes. I'll bring up your other suitcase after you've eaten."

"Great."

"Eat your soup before it cools. Call me when you're finished," Corey told him, walking out of the room.

His voice floated after her, its tone softly menacing. "You can be sure of that, Corey Hamilton."

She told herself the chills running up and down her spine were due to anger, but she didn't fool herself for a second. He interested her as no man ever had, and frightened her even more. Not physically, because she'd been trained in enough tricks to deal with anything, but emotionally. She feared him because she could not look at him dispassionately. He had shaken her safe little world in just a few minutes, and Corey wondered if her freedom was worth such a price. Slowly, she dredged up past discipline and past experiences that helped her make it through her years as an agent. Thankfully, most of her composure returned.

Corey was unpacking a crate of Japanese clocks when she felt someone watching her. Turning, she saw Matt approach. His rubber-tipped cane moved along as noiselessly as the tennis shoe that he now wore on his good foot. "What are you doing down here?" Corey asked, shaking pieces of pink and white Styrofoam out of her hair.

"I'm ready to talk." Matt announced, reluctantly admitting the attraction he felt for her. Only minutes before he had nearly convinced himself that Corey, though attractive, was not that special. But he had only to see her again, and he was lost, drawn to her by some strange, almost instinctual force.

"Go right ahead," Corey told him blandly. *He is*

just one more man, she told herself. *Nothing special*. "I've got to get these clocks unpacked so I can get rid of this packing junk. It's a real mess."

"No kidding?" Matt noted as he glanced around the room. It was littered with the stuff. "What is this? The crate looks Japanese, but these are American clocks, aren't they?"

"Both. They're genuine Japanese antiques, made in the 1890's to imitate our cheap American clocks," Corey explained, glad to turn the topic to clocks. She was comfortable with antiques and Matt looked genuinely interested in what she was saying. "The Japanese were into copying us earlier than you realize, professor. There are thousands of these clocks all over Japan, and probably even more in the US. They're worth considerably more in the States so I import them by the crate."

Corey relaxed when Matt proved to be a competent aide. He sat on a chair near her, his leg comfortably propped up. Corey unpacked each clock, removing its paper coverings then passing it on to Matt. He removed the inside paper, checking to make sure each had a pendulum. "Is this illegal, by any chance?" Matt finally asked with a teasing grin. His white teeth flashed in his dark face. If it hadn't been that question, Corey would have been fascinated by the change that occurred in his face when he smiled. "Are you selling clocks under false pretenses?"

"No. Whatever I am, I am honest. I tell people exactly what they're getting. Always." She stared at him with icy disdain, daring him to question her integrity again.

"What are you then, Corey?" Matt asked softly. "Do you run a halfway house for Parker? I don't understand your role in all this."

"That's two of us," Corey responded without thought. Then she held up her hand to forstall his speaking. "I said that I'd be honest with you, and I will be. You can ask me whatever you want. If it's related to your safety, I promise I'll answer. Other than that, it's on a need-to-know basis, and I may just tell you it's none of your business. Whichever, I won't lie."

"That sounds fair, Corey, more than fair," Matt murmured, wondering what emotions flickered beneath her polished veneer. "I promise to do the same. No lies between us." Wanting to touch her, he reached out to run his finger down her nose. As she forced herself not to pull from his touch, he wondered what made her so tense. Was it him or all men? Was it attraction she was fighting, or revulsion? Matt couldn't tell, and was all the more fascinated. Looking down into her blue eyes, he asked for the third time, "Who are you?"

Thinking seriously, Corey sat back, legs bent and feet crossed at the ankle, arms tightly clasped around them, and tried to answer as well as she could. "I'm an antique dealer now, but I did work for Parker. In electronics. I've been on leave for about a year. Parker made me an offer I couldn't refuse. I babysit you for a month and I'll be officially terminated."

"Terminated?" Matt asked, his eyebrows askew. "Isn't that another word for dead? Are you sure that you want to quit? Will your leaving the agency kill you?" Matt asked, wondering if that was a classic Freudian slip.

"Of course not," Corey replied carefully. She did want to end that part of her life, but she didn't think her life was over. It was merely going to begin again. "It's only semantics. I'll be officially retired."

"That is what you want?"

"Yes," Corey replied in a tone that announced that the subject was closed. "I'm more than competent to watch you, if that's what you're worried about. It's not the first time I've pulled bodyguard duty."

"I have no doubt about that at all, considering your actions this afternoon. You have great reflexes, Corey."

Before she could answer, Matt deliberately changed the topic. There was no rush. Before his month was over, Matt promised himself, he would understand everything about Corey Hamilton—and in the process, rid himself of his strange fascination with her. "So, where's your computer?" he asked, enjoying the momentary look of confusion that drifted across her face.

"Pardon," Corey said. "You want a computer? What for?"

"To write on. I brought my notebooks and cassettes with me, but I need a computer for the actual writing. I did a rough outline in the hospital. Don't tell me you don't have a computer? I thought every small business had one by now."

"Sorry. I haven't found any eighteenth- or nineteenth-century models that fit the decor. No trouble." Corey suddenly grinned. Nothing she liked better than to yank Parker's chain and mess up his beloved budget. "I'll buy one for you, and charge the agency. I know they want you to finish as soon as possible." Silently Corey added, *So do I.* The sooner Matt finished his book, the sooner he'd be safe. The sooner he would be gone.

"Tell me what you want and I'll get it by tomorrow. You look like you could stand a bit more sleep, so it should work out well.'' Corey jotted down Matt's requirements quickly, surprising him with her familiarity. ''I didn't say I didn't know how to use one, just that I don't have one.'' Pausing, Corey looked in Matt's bright eyes and was lost for a moment. An electric current seemed to flow between them, some mysterious attraction that Corey desperately needed to deny.

''So, Dr. Stone, we need to set some ground rules for your living here, once I get you all set up. I suggest that you spend most of your time upstairs.''

''All right. I am sort of grounded until the cast comes off anyway.''

Ignoring her curiosity about his leg, Corey added, ''You can have the empty bedroom. I'll bring up your meals.''

''I'll go crazy if I stay upstairs all the time. I insist on sharing meals with you. I'm not a bad cook, if I do say so myself.'' Tilting his head, he smiled in an adorable little-boy manner. ''C'mon, have some pity on an injured man.''

Waving her hands in agreement, she acquiesced against her better judgment. If Corey had her way, he'd stay in his room full-time and she'd never have to deal with the feelings he stirred up within her. Yet, she couldn't really expect him to stay cooped up all the time. It would be too much like jail. Much too confining for a man like this, one who was obviously used to an active lifestyle. No one had a body that was as lean and muscular as he did without some sort of regular exercise. Maybe she'd find out what his sport was, but not today.

''Fine. We'll share meals and you may come downstairs at night. But, during the shop hours, you stay upstairs. Out of sight.'' Corey breathed a sigh of relief when he nodded his head in agreement. So far Matt wasn't as unreasonable as Parker had suggested he would be.

"What are you going to tell the neighbors about me? Won't it ruin your reputation to have a man in your house?" Matt inquired, relieved that the living situation seemed to be working out so easily. "Someone will notice that I'm here sooner or later."

"Maybe, maybe not. None of my neighbors are close friends. If anyone asks, I'll tell them you're my cousin."

"Is that your usual excuse?"

"There is no usual excuse, Dr. Stone. You will be the first person who has stayed with me since I bought the place last year," Corey explained, quite aware that she was answering his unspoken question, though not quite sure why she bothered. "Except my sister and her kids. I told you I do not normally run a safe house. This is a one-time occurrence."

"Good," Matt murmured softly, pleased with the newly retrieved information. "So you've lived here for a year and have no boyfriends, or other male companions. Until now."

"Still, Dr. Stone. Still. You forget why you're here. In fact, if I don't get all the right papers by tomorrow, you'll be gone anyway," Corey announced, briefly forgetting that he had no knowledge of her agreement with Parker nor had any right to them.

"What do you mean, tomorrow? I thought it was all settled."

"Only if Parker keeps his word and sends me my termina—retirement papers."

"What's to keep you from kicking me out then?" Matt questioned, playing the role of devil's advocate.

He knew that he was goading her, but he couldn't help it.

"My word, Stone, just my word." Corey responded, turning to walk back into her combination storage and workroom. "Besides, my severance papers will probably arrive predated with your departure date. Parker always hedges a bet."

Awkwardly getting to his feet, Matt hobbled after her. "I'm sorry, Corey. I didn't mean it like it sounded. I want to stay so badly, I'm not reacting well."

Surprised, Corey turned back to face him. "Why?" It wasn't her business, but she suddenly had to know.

"I don't know, I just do!" Matt revealed, looking as puzzled by his reaction as she was. "I want to get to know you."

Turning his head back and forth, he missed her startled reaction as he raised one hand to his brow and ran a finger along both of his eyebrows, trying to verbalize his feelings. "I feel at home here, with you, for some crazy reason. Safe and settled, for the first time in nearly a year. I don't have to look over my shoulder. Is that enough?"

Suddenly looking up, he caught her gaze and their eyes locked. Some invisible communication moved between them. "You make me feel things I thought were gone," Matt reluctantly admitted. "Want things I'd forgotten I need. I plain want to stay. What else do you want?"

"Not that, Stone. What can I say to something like that? you've got the best line I've ever heard. So good," she slowly admitted, "that I'm not sure it's a line at all." Turning her back to him again, Corey walked over to pick up a small steeple clock that she had found last week at an estate auction. It was badly stained, and the veneer was in need of regluing. Staring at it, she chose her words carefully. "You'll be safe here, that I can promise you. The rest is probably due to your being overseas for so long. Coming back to the States after living in the Mideast is always a welcome shock to the psyche. Don't make more of it than it is. I'm just the first American woman that you've seen in a long time. You'd probably react this way to any woman you met. Go back upstairs and get some rest."

She was badly shaken by Matt's honesty. She wasn't used to men speaking their true feelings and she didn't think she liked it. Over her shoulder she again told Matt to go back upstairs and rest. "I'll get your computer set up. Help yourself to my books, if you want. Stay out of the shop. I'll go if the bell rings. I'll answer the phone." Not watching him leave, Corey bent over the clock. She felt she had made a momentous decision and hoped it was the right one. She should be done with this man and send him on his way, no matter what the cost. He could hurt her. She actually felt something for him.

Matt looked too tired, and the shadows under his eyes made her think he'd had nearly as much as he could take over the past few months. She could understand that. She would let him rest up, give him sanctuary while he healed. Then she'd send him back to his life, back to the sunny world of people who never made mistakes that killed. Without another thought, Corey walked to the phone.

Three hours later, Corey walked over to the window in her third bedroom with a great sense of satisfaction. On a sturdy oak table right in front of her sat an entire computer system, hooked up and operational. Matt would be pleased, she thought as she backed out of the room and tiptoed back down the stairs. She was relieved that Matt had slept through the serviceman's call. That was one less person to worry about.

Corey was writing up the memo she planned to send along with her receipt and the invoice to Parker when the doorbell rang. This was only the third customer to her shop that day, and just twenty minutes before it was supposed to close. Pushing her pen behind her ear, Corey looked up to see Mac, one of the agency's oldest and most reliable couriers. With a friendly smile, the older man gave her a thick manila envelope and several forms.

Turning to the side, she swiftly broke the seal on the envelope and pulled out the contents. The thick folder contained everything she'd requested: an official notice of retirement, a complicated medical policy that had Sean McCaulley's name on it, and more. Lots and lots more, Corey realized as she briefly leafed through the contents of the folder. It contained the rest of her personal papers, the personal tidbits and photos that she'd collected and retained at her desk back in DC. In its way, it was almost an album of her time at the agency. Compiled, no doubt, by Parker, and carefully designed to trigger her best memories and to remind her of the depth of her connection to the agency and himself. A note from Parker, telling her she was always welcome back at the agency was paperclipped to a picture of her standing on the beach at Nice, grinning happily at the camera. Parker's scrawl dared her to look over her past and then to walk away from it. Shoving the papers back into their envelope, she turned back to Mac.

"It's all there. Where's your pen?"

While she was signing the papers, Mac chatted amiably with her, not aware that he'd carried her severance papers with him. "So they've got you set up as an antique owner, have they? Last time I saw you, you were sitting in that truck in London."

"You know how it is. You never know where you're going to be from one week to the other in this business."

"Don't you know it," Mac replied as he turned and left.

Corey felt a sharp stab in her chest as he left, one that she didn't understand. Why didn't she feel triumphant? She'd hoped for this moment for the past year. After closing the shop, she picked up the thick envelope and held it, unaware that Matt was now standing quietly at the back of the shop.

Carefully, Corey walked into the living room and sat, cross-legged, in front of her fireplace. With a long match, she lit the kindling and watched it catch. She felt cold and needed to be near the warmth of the fire as she faced her past. Finally she withdrew a thick manila folder from the envelope on her lap.

"This is your life, Corey Winters Hamilton," Matt heard her whisper. "Damn you, Parker, for sending me all of this. I will not come back."

Corey opened the folder, searching for the medical policy. It was the single most important piece of paper in this montage. She scanned it slowly, deciding Parker had played fair with her. Sean was officially due medical benefits.

With a strange smile, Corey began to leaf through some of the other papers that Parker had included, wondering what his devious mind had thought would tempt her back. Parker had hinted to her, over and over again, that she'd miss the excitement of being an agent, never really realizing how much she'd hated it all.

As an expert in electronics, Corey had spent most of her time crouched in hot vans, or stealthily creeping around in the dark, placing various electronic devices in countless places. You name it and Corey had bugged it. She'd never been caught, never been involved in any actual physical confrontations until the very end, but the danger and stress had been constant and very real.

As her knowledge and sophistication increased, so did her tension. More and more she was aware of the consequences of her actions, both for the people that she "listened" to and for herself. They were all trapped in a grim world of deceit, lies, and danger. Only Corey's real patriotism and rare courage kept her functioning smoothly, hiding her terror from the rest of the world—especially from Parker.

Randomly she picked up an official-looking report, wondering if a document that shouldn't be there had been accidentally included in her papers. After a brief glance, Corey knew it had been no accident. Parker had stuck it in deliberately. It was the very first report on her, the agency's scouting report on her. Sighing, she saw a picture of herself at age sixteen standing next to her father and looking up at his strong face with an expression of worship. The folder noted her intelligence, her physical prowess, and the fact that she was already talking in terms of a career in the armed services. Corey remembered that year, when she was first approached by the agency. She always felt out of place in the twelfth grade, a smart girl who was two years younger than the rest. The agency's interest made her feel special and unique, and made her father so very proud of her. To serve her country and make her father proud of her. That had been her life until just last year.

As she sat motionless, caught in memories, Matt emerged from the shadows and quietly cleared his throat. "Are those the papers you were expecting?"

Starting, she turned to find his gentle eyes boring into her soul. "What do you want?" she demanded, closing the folder and hiding it against her chest. "What are you doing down here?"

"Those are the papers you were promised, aren't they? The ones that mean you're officially dismissed?" Matt asked her, walking slowly to her side. He sat in a chair nearest her, quietly insisting that she respond to him.

Corey answered, feeling trapped by his presence. "It's none of your business. Go away."

"Is everything there?"

"Yes. More than everything," Corey admitted, "Lots more than I expected." When Matt sat, quietly waiting, Corey found herself explaining. She needed to talk, had needed to share some of her experience for a very long time but had always denied that need, even to herself. Anger at Parker's deviousness added to the shock of her sudden freedom battered down her normal defenses.

"He sent my papers, all right, along with every picture or memento he could find to remind me of my glorious days as an agent. Even the scouting reports from when I was a kid. It's too bad that my father's dead, or Parker would have sent me a tape of him telling me to do the right thing."

"Sound like he wants you back pretty bad."

"He hates to waste things—anything. I still have expertise he can use. I invented a couple of electronic gadgets and he wants more. Most of all, he hates not to get his own way.''

''You really don't want to go back? How long have you been up here, fighting with him?''

''About a year,'' Corey admitted. ''Although I wasn't physically ready to go back until six months ago.''

''You were hurt?'' Matt asked gently, concern flowing from him to her, warming and soothing her pain.

Suddenly Corey realized that she was on the verge of talking to this near-stranger, really talking to him, and she froze. ''I'm fine now. All recovered. Perfectly able to protect you, professor.'' Standing up abruptly Corey sought to break the spell of intimacy that had mysteriously developed between them. She gathered the thick file up and put it back in the manila envelope. ''I'll put this away.''

When Corey returned, she found Matt sitting on the couch, staring pensively into the flames. Without thinking, without wondering what motivated her, Corey walked over to him and bonelessly collapsed next to him, staring into the fire.

Matt risked putting his arm around her shoulders, slowly pulling her toward him. Corey laid her head on the back of his arm, closing her eyes. ''I'm free,'' she murmured, ''finally free,'' before she burst into awkward, unaccustomed tears. Holding her tightly against him, Matt wondered what the cost of serving the government had been to this tender woman that she was so shaken by her freedom. Softly, he moved his hands up and down her back, soothing her. When she settled down and her sobs ceased, he offered her a large white handkerchief. With a curiosity born out of caring, and an intuitive knowledge that she needed to talk, Matt asked, "How long did you work for them?"

"Forever, Matt, forever," Corey sighed. She settled beside him, feeling safe, safe and cherished in a way that she'd forgotten. Not since she had been a small child, had she allowed herself to accept this type of physical comfort from anyone. That Matt was almost a stranger to her never entered her mind. He was there, safe and warm, and strangely caring. "Since I was sixteen."

"You're kidding me?" Matt said, his voice raised in surprise. "Our government doesn't recruit children!"

"I wasn't quite a child, Matt. I skipped two grades, so they first talked to me when I was in the twelfth grade. Parker surprised me with that little trip down memory lane to go along with my severance papers. It has my whole history in it, damn him. My whole life is in that envelope, every little bit." Corey lay back silently, resting her head on the cushion, letting Matt provide the comfort that she'd never sought before. Comfort that no one had ever offered before.

"It will be all right, Corey," his compassionate voice told her as he soothed her shoulders with warm palms. "Being free is not as hard as you think it will be."

Corey lifted her vulnerable eyes to his. "How did you know?" she asked.

"Changing your life hurts."

Minutes later, Corey stirred in his arms, sanity returning. She was dumbfounded at what she'd done, what she'd confessed to a near-stranger, let alone the man she was supposed to be protecting. For a few moments, their roles had been reversed and she'd felt sheltered in his arms. It was impossible, improbable, and all too enticing.

Schooling her face into impassivity, she pulled free from Matt, straightening her clothing as she stood up. "Thanks," she told him in a slightly husky voice. "I'll be in the workroom if you need me." With no further comment, she walked down the steps to her workshop and picked up the brass works of a clock.

Corey mechanically disassembled the brass gears, depositing them piece by piece into her untrasonic cleaning machine. As she worked, she tried to understand her strange reaction. In one hour she'd broken more taboos with this stranger than she had with any other living soul. Even the one time she'd thought herself madly in love, she'd never exposed her real feelings like she had today.

Finally, in desperation, she closed her eyes, resorting to the deep breathing techniques she'd used in the past to clear her mind. She couldn't count the number of hours she'd spent with this identical panicky feeling deep within her. It had been a constant factor, a sure sign that she was in serious danger.

Matt moved into the kitchen, thinking about his beautiful blond jailor while he cooked. Finally, he gave up. All he knew was that he liked this Corey Hamilton a lot, and that he wanted her more than he had any woman since his wife died.

When the timer rang, he matter-of-factly walked to the stairs and announced: "Dinner's ready."

As Corey entered the kitchen and washed her hands in the sink, she noticed he'd abandonded his cane.

"You shouldn't be walking like that. Where's your cane? They told me you were nearly helpless."

"Parker must enjoy exaggerating. I think he must have fudged the truth a little on both sides." Smiling, he adopted a terrible Mideastern accent, "Now, if you wanted immobile, you should have seen my first cast. The one I had in Israel was the real thing, complete with pullies and ropes and weights." Letting his voice slide back into its normal baritone, he gestured to his present cast. "This little gem is called a walking cast for very obvious reasons. I can get around pretty well, with or without the cane, but not for long periods of time. Nor with any speed. I think the fact that I was partially mobile was the only thing that saved me from Parker arresting me and putting me in a real jail."

"It wouldn't have been jail. Just protective custody."

"Would I or would I not have been locked away somewhere, unable to go out or do anything on my own?"

"More or less. In a nice apartment, with all the amenities."

"Well, it might have been a gilded jail," Matt hedged, "but a jail is a jail."

"This isn't that much different."

"This is a home, not a jail," Matt informed her firmly before he lightened the subject by adding, "Maybe it's because my jailor is so beautiful, and, besides, she lets me cook. Come on, dinner will get cold before we finish debating who is keeping whom company."

"Okay, but I'll cook tomorrow," Corey stated, moving so as to avoid touching him. It would be entirely too easy for her to become accustomed to his touch. Too easy and too addicting.

"Fine. Hurry up or you'll be eating cold Tuna Surprise."

"Did you say Tuna Surprise, as in tuna casserole?"

"Yep. I came from a big family, six brothers and sisters, and I know how to make every casserole known to modern man. Specialties of the house are tuna and hamburger. What's the matter, don't you like tuna fish? I did find it in your very own cupboard."

"Habit. Purely habit. Every time I go into a store I toss in a can without thinking. We ate a lot of tuna casseroles when I was growing up, too. The kindest thing to say about them is that they're not my first favorite food, or my second, either. But only a fool turns down a free dinner."

Minutes later, having consumed a large portion of the casserole, a bowl of salad, and a chunk of french bread, Corey leaned back in contentment. Somewhere during dinner, they had slipped into an easy conversation, light and amusing. Comfortable even, if Corey had allowed herself to label it. "What did you do to that tuna fish? I actually liked it!"

"Don't sound so surprised. It's my secret ingredient, Miss Hamilton."

Pausing for him to go on, Corey finally surrendered to her curiosity, as he hoped she would. "All right, Mister Chef, I give up. What's your secret ingredient?"

"Promise you won't tell the world? They might create a shortage of tuna and—"

Corey interrupted him with a laugh. "I swear I won't tell. It'll be top secret."

Leaning over, Matt whispered in her ear, "Almonds."

"Almonds? You put almonds in a tuna casserole?"

"Surprised you, didn't I?"

"Well, it did taste all right," Corey admitted. "Now I can't wait to see what you do to liver, my other all-time favorite."

"You win, Corey." Matt laughed, "No one can make liver taste good, no matter what you add."

"You cooked, so I'll clean up," Corey told him as they smiled tentatively at each other. Abruptly, she stood and began to stack their plates. "Go sit down and have a brandy. I'll join you soon."

Corey cleaned up the dinner dishes slowly, confused by the light, pleasant meal. Matt was not what she expected. Anybody else would have questioned her. Matt asked her nothing. He'd held her and let her tears wash through the pain, given her what she needed without question, demanded no repayment. Yet.

Now it was time to find out what sort of price she would be asked to pay for his consideration. Perhaps he was a superb game-player, and this was a subtle variation of the rules. Corey almost hoped that Matt would make a real pass at her, thereby doing something that she most certainly could handle. Whatever happened, their relationship was not going to be casual. Too much had already happened between them. Somehow they had to mold rules to get them through this next month, and, Corey reminded herself, let her wave good-bye to him without regret.

Straightening her shoulders, Corey marched into the living room, as though she were facing an inquisition. Matt smiled when he saw her. His keen peripheral vision gave him an advantage at times like this. He smiled to himself as he watched her take a deep breath before coming to stand in front of him. Before she could say anything, he disarmed her.

"Thank you for the computer system. It's exactly what I needed."

"I'm glad."

"I'll be able to get started tomorrow."

"Good." Corey cleared her throat, absently twirling her brandy within its deep glass. "We need to set up some rules."

"More rules?" Matt questioned with a quirked eyebrow. "All right. You're the expert. What more do you think we need? I already have the idea that I'm not supposed to do anything or go anywhere without your express permission. I already agreed to that. Let me ask you some questions, though. Can I go out once in a while for a breath of fresh air, maybe at night? No one can stay inside one place, no matter how cozy, for four weeks without going stir crazy. Perhaps we could drive around some? I'd like to see some of Cape Cod while I'm here."

"You're here to write, not vacation. You can come back and see the sights after you turn in your book. Promise me that you won't go out without me, anywhere. Remember, you wouldn't be here if Parker didn't think that you needed me . . ." Corey paused briefly and refocused. "That is, that there was a real threat."

"I do need you, in many many ways."

Corey steeled herself and looked directly into Matt's blue eyes. "I don't want to get involved. I won't. This is a purely professional relationship."

"I know what it's supposed to be, but it's too late for that. We are already involved. From the moment that we first saw each other."

"No, we are not! You don't know anything about me." Looking up into his heated gaze, Corey spoke the truth. "Look, you were a real nice guy tonight, not making a pass at me, but that's it."

When Matt shook his head, denying her words, Corey went on. "All right. I admit that I'm not totally indifferent to you, I don't imagine many women in the world are. You're a sexy man. One sex-starved man, if I know anything about the Mideast. You told me yourself, you're just back in the country. I'm the first woman you've spent any time alone with. Think about it. You'd feel this way about any moderately attractive woman." When Matt again shook his head, Corey went on in a slightly desperate tone. "All right. Maybe, maybe, we have some strange chemical attraction to each other. But that is it. It can't be anything else and it can't go anywhere."

"Are you asking me to stop wanting you?"

"I'm telling you that you can't have me."

"N-oo?" Matt drawled, hauling himself up to walk over to her chair. Leaning his hip against the back of the chair, he pulled her up so that Corey was resting on her knees, facing the back of the chair. Their bodies met just above the waist, her firm breasts crushed against his cotton shirt. Pulling her into his arms, Matt slowly bent down to touch the edge of her lip with his tongue.

Corey turned, ready to move away from the chair when he touched her, but something held her. When the tip of his tongue touched her lips, the tenderness of his embrace caught her in its sensual web. Corey relaxed, accepting his kiss, the gentle worship of lips and tongue. Slowly, delicately, Matt deepened the kiss, seeking her sweetness, calling forth her hidden need. Her mouth opened to him, granting him access. His tongue plundered, rushing to taste and touch all with a wild passion.

Melting, Corey leaned into the chair for support. His touch rekindled feelings that she had thought long dead. It insisted she remember the growing ache that she knew from past experience would never be fully satisfied.

Suddenly she felt strong hands running over her face, and felt the shock of rough material against her cheek. Matt had pulled her down to cling to his chest, softly laughing when she instinctively moaned in protest. "It's too soon," he told her, soothing the fires that he just ignited, instead of fanning them to fruition. "Just don't ever lie to yourself about us. All the rules in the world can't stop this."

When Corey tensed, ready again to struggle, humiliated and furious as she emerged from the sensual web that he'd trapped her in, his hands were like iron on hers. "Stop it, Corey," Matt ordered before she began to use her training to free herself. "I don't doubt you could throw me over the room if you wanted to, but I've already got one broken leg. You can do the other one when this one's healed." Cautiously letting her go, he bent down to catch her eye. "I want to talk."

"You want, you want, you want. Well, Mister Doctor Matthew Stone, let me tell you what I want." She moved stiffly over to the fireplace before turning to confront him. With a coolness that was belied by her rapid breathing, she informed him, "I don't want you to touch me again. Ever."

"Corey, my sweet," Matt chided her softly. "We just proved, to the contrary, that you want me to touch you. Or do you react that way when anyone kisses you? Be honest, that's all I ask."

"No," Corey said slowly, telling him the truth, but not the entire truth. She had never responded to anyone the way she responded to him. "But it doesn't mean anything. You're obviously an expert. We're both lonely, that's all."

Laughing, Matt looked at her. "You won't quit fighting it, will you?"

"Never. Look, just tell me what you want."

"I want to get to know you. I want us to be friends. Ultimately, we will be lovers, too, but only when you're ready. I'd never force you, even if I could."

"That's all this . . . this macho display was about? You want to be friends?" Snorting, Corey let her anger speak, searching for any excuse for Matt's behavior that excluded her. "Honesty is what you want? Fine. What about the explanation for your behavior? I think this little display might have been caused by something different than attraction, than wanting to be friends. Maybe you're not comfortable with a woman who can throw you over her shoulder. You sure were surprised this morning when I turned out to be Corey Hamilton and when I pinned you up on the bed. Maybe you don't want a woman to protect you. Just maybe your inflated male ego took over and figured you'd even things up. I could protect you, you could seduce me. Sex would even up the equation, SOP."

"You think that this is *my* standard operating procedure? All because my male ego is threatened by you?"

"Well . . ."

"No, lady. It's not. I haven't chased a woman like this since I first met Sally." Matt broke off in midsentence and his face changed, a mask falling over it, hiding the thoughts that suddenly swirled in his head. Why did this one blond woman remind him of his late wife, his delicate raven-haired wife? They were nothing alike.

"You're right," Matt said briskly a moment later. "I was way out of line. Maybe it was ego. I've never been in a situation like this before. And, like it or not, I will admit that I've been more frightened in the last few months than ever before. They say that fear is a natural aphrodisiac. Did you find it so in your job?" Matt asked politely, moving back to the couch and retrieving his brandy. He took a quick gulp, hoping that he had his emotions back in control.

Swallowing her surprise, Corey realized the passionate man who kissed her was gone. The remote, slightly insulting stranger who entered her shop twelve hours ago was back again. It was for the best.

"No, I did not," Corey announced coldly. "In case you had your hopes up, sexual favors do not come with the room, board, and protection. Nor did they ever. I accept your apology, such as it is, as long as you keep your hands off. We've got to cope for a month, so you do your writing, and I'll keep you safe. And I don't want to discuss my past. It's none of your business nor is it relevant to our professional agreement."

Matt remained silent, sorry that he had taken such a cheap shot at her but still stunned by her response to him. Her kiss had been too sweetly inexperienced, her responses too full of wonder. He had expected experience, even decadence, in her touch but had found the exact opposite. It had been fear that caused him to pull back, but not the fear she imagined he was referring to. It was his fear of his own feelings and his reaction to the emotions that she reawakened in him. He was willing to drop the subject for the present. But Matt knew that her past was relevant, and unfortunately so was his. Sooner or later, they would discuss it all.

He stood quietly, watching Corey walk around, turning down the lights. "I'll show you my security system in the morning, Matt. Tonight, don't come downstairs alone. This place is pretty secure. As I said, electronic devices were my specialty. It's probably why Parker thought of me in the first place."

As she followed him up the stairs she could not help but admire the firmness of his buttocks in his faded jeans. His legs were long and muscular, and he negotiated the stairs with surprising ease. "Hey, professor," she found herself asking, "Parker never told me how much longer you'll need that cast."

"This one's been on for almost a week. I'm due to have it removed in three weeks, so the last part of our visit should be easier on us all."

"I sincerely hope so," Corey told him as he disappeared into his door.

An uneasy truce existed between Corey and Stone the next morning. They both felt raw and awkward with each other. Corey brought him his breakfast on a tray and escaped after a few formal words of greeting. She heard the intermittent sound of printing drift down from his computer during the morning. Surprisingly, the sounds of someone else in the house gave her comfort. She must have been alone too long. Accordingly, she made a note on her calendar to buy a cat as soon as Stone left.

Several tourists wandered in that morning. Clear and sunny spring weather usually brought them out to the Cape's shoreline. Casually, Corey managed to always stay between them and the door to her living quarters. Once she had to tell a young man politely that the shop did not extend behind the door. She looked over each tourist in a professional way. Only after she gauged them harmless, did she react to them as a shopkeeper.

Her fifth batch of customers for the day was an older couple and their teenage daughter, who purchased one of the inexpensive Japanese clocks. After they left the store, Corey put out the Closed For Lunch sign and walked to the kitchen, thinking deeply of the morning just past. She was bemused by her own reactions and surprised by the tension that she felt in her neck. This is the way she'd lived for ten years. She'd partially forgotten the constant tension, the never-ending alertness that was part of her everyday life as an agent. Probing her mind for the truth, Corey finally gave a long sigh of relief.

She had been right and Parker wrong. She had not secretly liked the danger and fear, she did not need to live on the edge. She didn't miss it one little bit. It would be hard to maintain the old vigilance for the next month. Her year away from the agency had worked. She was really a civilian—or at least she would be once this month with Stone was over.

When lunch was ready, Corey put it on a tray and carried it up the stairs. She was quietly contented, pleased that she'd been correct about her own feelings. As she approached the door, she felt an involuntary laugh escape before she controlled herself. Posted with two push pins was a long computer printout that proclaimed the trite but never more true words: "TODAY IS THE FIRST DAY OF THE REST OF *OUR* LIFE."

Chills rushed over his spine as Matt heard the low, sultry laughter that announced Corey's entrance. He barely had time to wipe the hunger off his face before she appeared with his tray.

"So, you like my sign?"

"We are talking trite here, really, really trite. But somehow it's true. How did you know that I felt just that way?"

"What do you mean?"

"I was down in the shop today, doing the whole surveillance routine. And I found that I didn't miss doing it one little bit. I really am a civilian."

"I'm sorry then that I'm here. Will it bother you to guard me?"

"What? No. No. It's no trouble. It's not that I mind doing it, it's just that I'm so glad that I don't miss the tension and the feelings that come with being so . . . so alert. I can still do it, but I don't need it. I'm happier when I'm just being a plain antique dealer."

"I'm glad for you, although I refuse to ever think of you as plain. Then this really is a new beginning. Can we begin together, too?" Matt offered. "Friends for now?"

Her heart burst into a fluttered pounding as Matt reached toward her. When his hand traced a line on her face, Corey felt the now familiar excitement fizz in her blood, the warmth of his touch affecting her like champagne. This man was a walking time bomb. He could turn her to mush with one touch. Shaken, Corey turned her stunned blue eyes up to stare at him. "I don't know, Matt. You affect me, you scare me." Turning, she walked to the window. "I still won't go to bed with you," she told him.

"I'll never hurt you, Corey," Matt promised, touched by her honesty and pleased by her feelings. He wasn't absolutely sure what to call his feelings for her, but he knew that they were real. "I will never hurt you."

"Not on purpose, Matt," Corey admitted. "But you don't know me. You can't promise what you don't know."

"Yes, I can," Matt said steadily. "We'll get to know each other. I'll keep my hands to myself. No more passes."

"Okay," Corey agreed, knowing she was lying to herself, but having very little choice in the matter. She knew she was sinking deeper and deeper into the quicksand that was Matt Stone, but he was there in her life and she couldn't ignore him. No one was that strong or that dumb. "We can't stay like this, walking on pins and needles with each other. It's too hard on us both." Sticking her hand out for a shake, "Friends it is," she said.

Matt gave her hand a brief shake, trying to be as friend-like as possible. It didn't stop him from enjoying the soft touch of her skin, nor did it stop Corey from reacting to his touch all the way to her toes. "We're dynamite, Corey," Matt murmured, unable to restrain the tremble that raced from his hand to hers. "But we won't explode unless you're ready." Feeling less than reassured, Corey left the room.

A cautious truce existed between them over the next few days. They both had internally acknowledged that their attraction was almost irresistible, so they tried very hard to avoid physical contact with each other. Matt worked at his word processor during the day, making a great deal of progess. The passion that he was controlling spilled over into his writing.

The nights evolved into an easy camaraderie. They fixed dinner together. Corey insisted that Matt produce at least one more of his world-famous casseroles, though based on hamburger this time. They talked long and hard about a wide range of subjects. One night they toured her shop. Corey stopping here and there to give the history of her best pieces.

"Corey," Matt announced. "You are a romantic."

"It was as much a surprise to me as it is to you. Not a very sensible trait for someone in my old line of work."

"How did you ever become an agent, Corey? I can't imagine that they had a booth at career day at your high school."

Matt took her hand and pulled her gently but persistently behind him until they were settled on the couch in her living room.

"If I tell you the story of Corey Hamilton, agent, will you tell me the story of Matt Stone, professor and author? How did you manage to get a bunch of bloodthirsty Syrians chasing you?"

"Deal, Corey," Matt agreed, almost before she could finish her sentence. He was pleased beyond belief that she was willing to share some of her life with him and had actually volunteered to deepen their relationship. "But not all in one night. Tomorrow we'll start the Matthew Stone saga. Tonight we can find out how you went from Girl Scout to girl spy."

Corey slowly nodded, aware that their relationship had gradually changed. She trusted him now. She liked him now. The four days that they spent together told her what kind of man Matt was. She'd seen him grouchy in the morning and tired at night. She could see the restlessness come over him, and the longing to walk out in the fresh air. She saw him lose his temper in complete frustration one day when the electricity unexpectedly went off and he'd lost forever several pages of his manuscript. He was a nice man, kind and good and sensitive, and Corey found herself drawn to him. Even though she knew their time was limited, Corey decided to enjoy whatever she could have with Matt, hoping their friendship could persevere. Now that she wasn't an agent, she could have regular friends.

"What did you first dream of doing?" Matt questioned softly. "I don't imagine that you started out wanting to be an agent?"

"No, not quite, though I did have my share of fantasies that I'd be a detective someday. Mostly, I wanted to be a pilot, like my dad. He was Navy, career Navy, and one of the best pilots ever. I was pretty much of a tomboy. I was never much interested in the dolls and stuff my sister was. I was going to be the very first female fighter pilot."

"And . . ."

"A man like Parker showed up. They'd been watching me for a couple of years before they contacted me. They like to recruit from military families, it makes the backgrounds verifiable. Anyway, in my senior year, a man like Parker, a smiling, genial man, came to talk to my father and me. They offered to pay for college and give me a job that involved travel, excitement, and a chance to help my country. How could I refuse?"

"No way," Matt said softly, reaching out to touch her shoulder. "They didn't see the sensitive girl, did they? They only saw your father's daughter."

"To be fair, Matt, that is all I let them see. Maybe that was all there was then. I was very glad to serve my country. I still don't regret my time with the agency," Corey heard herself saying, slightly surprised to find that it was true. Sometime in the past year, she had let go of her anger and began to accept her past for what it was. "They were very good to me. I've been trained to protect myself. I speak four languages fluently and know enough electronics to open my own shop, if I wanted. I told you that my specialty was in electronic eavesdropping."

A silence filled the air as Matt digested what Corey had revealed. "Then why did you stop?"

"At first it was like a game, and I was always the good guy. It was all kind of unreal. Other people got me in and out, then left me alone to do my job. Most of it was at night or in the dark, sneaking around when no one was there, planting my equipment and then monitoring it from some safe, quiet place. I saw very little of what you'd call 'direct action.' I observed it all, recording, listening, but never really involved."

Focusing on the fire, she went on. "More and more, though, the black and white became shades of gray." Swallowing, Corey decided to be honest, with Matt and herself. Maybe it was time to talk about her real feelings with someone. "After a couple of years I realized that what I'd thought was excitement wasn't. It was fear. I spent most of my time listening to secrets, sick to my stomach and trying not to show it. I never told anyone. Finally I made a decision that I couldn't live with."

"What happened?"

"I . . . I can't talk about it."

Seeing her pain, Matt changed topics, asking her a more general question about the Mideast. Two hours later, Matt looked at Corey in shock. He was stunned by her knowledge and understanding. "Would you be willing to read my manuscript and add a couple of the anecdotes you told me? Your insights will make it stronger."

"I'd be glad to." More than glad, she admitted to herself. His offer for her to read and even add to his book was more important to her than one to share his bed, because it was an honest offer, based on mutual respect. "I'd be honored."

"Good," Matt said solemnly, as though they'd exchanged a vow. "I'll hold you to that." Ruffling her curly head, he changed the mood and said, "Let's go to bed. You've got a business to run and I've got a book to write. It's two o'clock in the morning, if you didn't notice."

Matt headed upstairs as Corey checked the alarms and turned off the lights. She caught up with him as he was entering his bedroom, and impulsively she reached up to plant a soft kiss on his lips. "Thank you for tonight."

With restraint, Matt watched her enter her room, wanting nothing more than to take her in his arms and finish the night in the proper manner. Not tonight, he promised himself, but soon he would have her.

FOUR

Corey awakened slowly the next morning, unusually reluctant to abandon the warm comfort of a deep sleep. The persistent buzz of her alarm finally forced her to stumble out of bed long enough to hit the off button. Standing near the wall, she battled the urge to run back and burrow under the covers when she realized it was already nine. Not only had she overslept, but she had done it on a Saturday, her busiest day.

Sprinting into the hall toward the bathroom, Corey ran full tilt into Matt's bare chest, a warm muscular wall that didn't move. Corey gasped, looking straight at a bronzed chest whose well-defined muscles were covered with a dark triangle of soft hair. Black curls barely covered his small masculine nipples, dusting his chest in a soft cover. Resisting an unwelcome impulse to touch those soft curls, Corey backed up, starting to apologize as she automatically lowered her eyes.

Unfortunately that view was no less distracting. Matt was wearing a pair of very loose pajama bottoms, tied low on his hips. Her eyes involuntarily followed the arrow of black curls as it narrowed at

55

his trim waist and then began to widen again, just before it disappeared beneath the blue material. Forcing her eyes up, she stared into Matt's knowing eyes as she cleared her throat and managed to say, ''Good morning'' in an almost steady voice.

When Matt noticed Corey's door opening, he'd barely had time to brace himself against the doorjamb before she ran into him. She was wearing a floor-length confection of lace and silk, sheer enough that it left little to the imagination. He'd suspected that her figure was remarkable, but this was the first time that he was able to see her without the folds of the heavy sweaters that she favored wearing. Her breasts were perfect, firm and high, slightly more voluptuous than he expected. Their rosy tips were shadowy temptations through the pale-beige silk as was the slight suggestion of gold that flickered into his view between her long, lean legs.

Unable to resist, Matt reached down to gather her close to him. ''Good morning to you,'' he returned before his lips descended on hers, pulling her against his fully aroused body. Using the wall as balance, Matt put one firm hand behind Corey's back and fitted her to him.

Before Corey could do more than tighten her muscles in preparation for flight, Matt had captured her with his passion. Their mouths melted together. Sweetness blended with passion as they explored the fire that they created. Finally Corey collapsed against Matt in near surrender. Needs that she had long forgotten came to the surface, along with others that were entirely new.

The urgency of her feelings finally brought Corey out of her stupor. Desperately she forced herself to pull away. Her resistance brought Matt back to reality and he realized just how close he had been to taking her in the hall, at that very moment. As much as he wanted that, Matt knew it would be the end of them, for Corey was not ready.

Panting, he stood up straight, and held her tight against him, struggling to control his breathing. "Let me hold you, Corey honey, for a minute. I can't let you go yet, not yet," he crooned, needing her touch, knowing that he would feel bereft as soon as their bodies parted. Thankfully, he felt her relax at his words. "That's some kiss, lady," he finally said as he let her go and she moved back from him.

"Oh, Matt," Corey groaned, too aroused and too frightened to hide behind any pretense. "You scare me to death. I don't know what to do. You make me feel things I thought were dead. Things I don't want to feel."

As her passion cooled, her anger grew—anger at herself for responding and at Matt for making her want the forbidden. "This whole thing has to stop!" She took a deep breath and stared directly into his eyes. "I don't want any of this. I won't like you, Stone. I don't want to want you. I absolutely refuse to have any sort of sexual relationship with you. So you've got two choices in this. Either you keep this association strictly professional or I'll lock you in this room until your book is done. Your choice."

"Are you that afraid of me?" Matt asked in a bemused tone. "You know you could knock me out in two seconds flat. You're afraid of yourself and blame me for it," he accused with cruel accuracy.

Corey ignored his answer and repeated her terms. "Either keep your hands off, or I'll lock you up in here." He had no right playing amateur psychologist. She refused to give him the satisfaction of admitting that he was right. It was her reaction that she was afraid of, not his.

"It won't work, you know," Matt said in a lighter tone. "You can't pretend that we don't care for each other. I can't stop wanting you, or liking you. I refuse to even try."

"You don't know anything about me," Corey snapped despite herself. "How can you like me when you don't know what my life was like, what I was, what I've done?"

"It doesn't matter. I know what you are now, and that's all that matters to me. I have a past, too, and some baggage that I don't much like." Softly, Matt added, "We all do."

Leaning back, Corey took a moment to think. She did like Matt, it was impossible to deny that. And he was unreasonably sexy. But she'd handled tougher assignments than this one. The only reason that she reacted so strongly to Matt's embrace was that she'd been half asleep. "One last chance, then. I won't change the rules if you don't. No more kisses or you're confined to quarters. We're friends, no more."

"I promise that we'll be friends, Corey. The rest we can play by ear," Matt noted over his shoulder as he sauntered into his bedroom, as well as any man with a cast can saunter. "Hadn't you better get dressed? It's after nine-thirty."

By 5:30 Corey was bone-tired and restless, an unusual combination for her. She had been exceptionally busy at the shop that day. The sunny day had brought out several Bostonians, and she'd sold a dining-room table with matching chairs for a very good price. She felt in need of a celebration.

Normally after a day like this, she would drive

over to visit her godfather and spirit him out of his nursing home for a quick meal. Sean was an important part of Corey's life. As her godfather, he had participated in most of the important occasions in her life, as well as providing support during the terrible times when she had to face the death of not only her grandparents but her mother as well. He was the only "family" that she had left besides a married sister who lived in New Jersey. Lost in thought, she started when Matt's voice came down the stairway, peering into the darkened shop. "All done?"

"Yeah. Let me finish locking up." Turning, Corey recalled a conversation they'd had a couple of days after Matt had moved into her shop. As he watched her set her alarm system, Matt had asked, "Why such elaborate locks, Corey?"

Matt had been more than mildly surprised when he was given a guided tour of Corey's security system. It had everything from double-strength glass to an electronic number-coded lock to motion sensors on all the windows. Though Corey had shrugged off the question, Matt had persisted. "Why so much security, Corey? I've seen museums with less."

"Habit, I guess. I told you that electronics was my specialty. I helped design and install the security for quite a few of our embassies. Anyhow, when I moved in here, there was nothing but a joke of a lock. I started with the deadbolts and then I just kept adding systems until I felt safe. I made most of it myself, as a hobby."

"It makes sense. With your expertise." Suddenly, he had another thought. "I don't imagine that you were able to totally relax very many times when you were overseas and you needed a safe place to hide."

Sighing in acknowledgment of his insight, Corey

lost another tiny piece of her heart. "You do understand. No one else does. Even Parker thought I was silly. He kept telling me that I was paranoid, especially when I ordered the heavy glass. He thought it was another symptom of my burn-out."

"He's the foolish one, not you. I'd have done the very same thing."

Her mind returned to the present when she heard Matt calling her name. "Is there any way we could get out of here for a little while? It's Saturday night, and I have a terrible urge for a nice fresh lobster. I promise to do whatever you say."

"Why not?" Corey replied recklessly. "No one's shown up all week, and it's pretty dark by now. I know a perfect place."

"Shall I change?" Matt asked, indicating his jeans and casual fisherman's knit sweater.

"Yeah. Age ten years and put on twenty pounds," Corey teased with a devilish smile before she told him to put on a pair of sweatpants so that no one could see his cast. "This place has a certain, shall we say ambiance? And I promise you, no Middle Easterner would ever be seen there," Corey laughed. Only the inhabitants of the Cape frequented the restaurant, its extremely shabby facade putting off all but the most adventurous of tourists.

Her lovely face was full of mischief, and Matt realized that he'd seen, for a brief moment, the younger Corey, the girl who had existed before the agency taught her to mistrust her own instincts. What had happened to change her, he wondered as he walked up the stairs. She must have seen a lot of things in her ten years with Parker, and Matt was willing to bet that many of them were unpleasant and some of them outright dangerous. A cold chill ran through him as he thought of Corey in danger. A picture of a gun or a knife held near her made him feel ill. Suddenly he laughed aloud. How could a man feel protective in the past tense? Whatever happened, she had obviously survived.

Shoving an old sweatshirt over his muscular shoulders to match the soft gray cotton pants that he'd already donned, Matt hobbled down the stairs to find Corey waiting for him, dressed in a shabby black sweatsuit and old tennis shoes.

"You wanted to make our first date memorable, so you dressed up as fancy as you knew how."

"You rat. I'll have you know I could knock your socks off if I put on my fancy stuff."

"No need, Corey. You already knocked them off days ago."

"And this is not a date. It's dinner," Corey countered.

"If you say so."

"Do you think it's safe to go out?" Matt asked as he caught sight of the small gun that Corey had stuck in her purse. "I don't want to endanger you. All the danger and deceit seem so unreal here. I forgot the terrorists and their guns for a while, and the fact that this is not pretend."

"I think we'll be all right. If anyone was out there, we would have noticed them by now. I think we can safely assume that you are 'hidden.' I wouldn't agree otherwise."

"I trust you, Corey."

With that, Corey got up and walked to the back door. "Wait here. I'll drive around and pick you up."

Matt sat on the back porch amusing himself by imagining what sort of car Corey would drive. He had ruled out several sportscars when he saw a medium-sized Chevrolet station wagon edging around the alley. It was light blue, and looked like several million other cars.

Laughing, Matt got in the front door. When she demanded to know what was so funny, Matt said, "I was imagining what sort of car you would drive, working my way through the exotic, fast models when you show up in this. I was expecting glitz and glamour and I got practical."

"What's wrong with this? It's a good car."

Matt cut her off with another deep chuckle. "You don't have to defend your car to me. I know exactly what it is, I should have guessed. It's fast, efficient, and inconspicuous. A perfect car for a government worker, or an undercover agent? Right?"

"It is perfectly practical, especially if you haul furniture around like I do. Besides, I'd feel silly in a bright-red Ferrari. Even if I could afford it."

"Is it really the money?" Matt probed. "Would you feel silly in a fast car, Corey, or is this just the car you think every good agent should drive?"

"All of the above, I suppose." Corey admitted with a sigh. "I'm used to cars like this, ones that blend into the crowd."

"Didn't you ever want a fast car, something special, even as a teenager?" Matt asked, wanting to know anything at all about her past, no matter how trivial.

Driving down the misty road, Corey admitted that as a teenager she harbored a secret desire for a canary-yellow MG-midgit convertible. "Once, they were in a pinch and I was put into the field for three weeks in Hamburg pretending to be a rich American, and they gave me a Ferrari to drive. That was a real kick,

especially over in Germany where there are no speed
limits. That was a fantastic month. Nothing bad happened. I didn't have to do anything at all but live the
good life until they found out it was a false alarm. I
really missed that car when it was over.'' Suddenly
Corey bit her tongue and threw a desperate glance
toward Matt's interested face. ''I don't know where
that came from. I've never mentioned my work to
anyone outside the business before. I never, never
talk without thinking. It's not allowed.''

''You're outside the business now,'' Matt reminded
her softly. ''You don't have to follow their rules
now. You can make up your own.''

''Not really. There are lots of things I can't talk
about. Things are still classified. And probably always will be.''

''Besides those special incidents, the rest of your
memories are your own. You didn't tell me anything
that could possibly be secret, did you?''

''Well, no.''

''Then don't worry about it. Besides, I'm a perfectly safe person to confide in. I have some sort of
agency approval and passed some security check or I
wouldn't be here.''

Corey braked to a stop in front of a building that
looked like a run-down open-air market. ''We're
here,'' she announced gratefully. Their conversation
was getting out of hand, as it too often seemed to
with Matt. Corey didn't want to know why she'd
impulsively told Matt anything at all. ''You stay in
the car, and I'll be back in a few minutes with
dinner. There's a spot down the beach where we can
sit at a picnic table, if it's not too chilly for you?''

''That would be great.'' What Matt needed most
was some fresh air and a feeling that he wasn't

trapped by four walls. The night was cool but not cold. It was neither too windy nor too foggy for them to enjoy the darkness. Matt knew that the temperature had nothing to do with the heat that he felt flare within him.

A half hour later they were seated on a picnic bench, sitting comfortably together, thighs touching, lobster shells scattered in front of them. Corey bought two lobsters each, as well as several side orders of potato salad, cole slaw, french fries and, off to the side, two pieces of Art's special blueberry cheesecake. A bottle of white wine drunk in paper cups added a last touch.

They munched together comfortably, uncaring that the lobsters were messy or that they occasionally squirted the other with a splash of juice when a stubborn claw or tail broke open. After the major portions of all four lobsters had been consumed, they leaned back and grinned at each other.

"You've done this before," Corey accused. "You eat lobster like an old New Englander."

"I was born in Maine, so I've been eating lobsters longer than you, I imagine."

"Are you asking me how old I am in a roundabout manner?"

"Would you tell me?"

"Why ever not? I'm twenty-nine. How about you?"

"Thirty-five. Didn't Parker tell you?

"No, he told me very little about you beyond a thumbnail sketch of your past and a more detailed one about your problem. I had the impression that you'd be an old white-haired professor who I'd have to nursemaid around. If Parker had told me what you were like, I'd probably have refused, no matter what he offered."

"Smart man, that Parker," Matt murmured. "So," he said, tracing a finger along the line of Corey's brows, "finish your story. I know how the agency recruited you, know that you can't tell me everything about your time with them, but I still haven't heard how you ended up in Cape Cod as an antique dealer."

"My godfather, Sean McCaulley, owned the shop before I did. When I got . . ." Corey stopped herself from saying, "out of the hospital" and substituted instead "back to the States . . . I dropped in to see him. He's all the family I have left, aside from a younger sister in New Jersey. He has no other family, either, so we've been close for years."

Corey looked off into the ocean, and then continued in an expressionless voice. "I was pretty shaken up when I came back, and Sean didn't ask any questions. Just gave me a room and told me to stay as long as I wanted to. Anyway, he's seventy-nine, and about three weeks after I got here, he had a stroke. Luckily I was with him and got him to the hospital in time. He's pretty much recovered, but it forced him to move into a combination nursing home and retirement village. I wanted to keep him with me, at the shop, but the doctors said he needed round-the-clock nurses available. So I bought out his shop. It worked out pretty well for us both."

Shivering, Corey turned to Matt and told him it was time to return. The breeze had picked up, but it wasn't that cold wind that made her shiver. It was the company. Why did she open up to Matt? Why did she feel so safe with this man? She could not allow herself to feel anything for Matt. He would be gone in two and a half weeks. That was the essential fact. No matter what her traitorous body was telling her, she was not going to be drawn into some half-baked affair that would be over in two weeks. It simply was not her style.

She gathered up the leftovers, neatly putting the salads into one bag, along with the bodies of the lobsters to be picked clean later for a midnight snack. When Corey's hand collided with Matt's, both reaching for the lobster remains, she laughed. "You are a native. No one else bothers with the meat in the body and small legs." Graciously, she told him they could share the legs later. "We can have the cheesecake at home, with coffee," she told him as she opened her car door.

Matt almost smiled as he began to recognize a pattern in Corey's behavior. Each time she shared a little more with him, each time she opened up, she immediately retreated. The professional woman came back, mask in place, but now Matt wasn't too concerned. Someday he would find a way to remove that mask entirely, and then she would be his.

"I'll go and get my husband to carry it to the car, my dear," an elderly customer announced the next morning just before they both heard a terrible crash from upstairs.

"What was that?" the woman asked, as Corey started.

"I don't know. It sounds like something fell over. If you'll excuse me," Corey said, rushing the woman out the door. "I'll give you the clock and go up to see what happened." Before the woman could reply, Corey had the woman and the clock on her front step, her door locked, and she was bounding up the stairs.

"Matt, are you all right? What happened?" she demanded as she glanced into the open door of her empty bedroom. "Where are you?" Corey repeated as she rushed to the computer room. When that proved empty, she gave the bathroom door a sharp knock.

"I'm coming in, Matt, if you don't answer me immediately." All Corey heard was a moan. She turned the handle and found the door locked. "Fool," she muttered as she stepped back into the hall and took a second to improve her concentration. With a quick leap, she used a karate kick that she'd learned long ago to hit the door just next to the lock. The sudden pressure broke the lock and the door sprang open, barely missing Matt's head. He was sprawled on the tile floor, his head resting squarely on the fluffy bathroom rug. He was soaking wet, completely naked, and somewhat dazed. The water was still running from the showerhead onto his lower body. Corey quickly turned off the water and knelt beside Matt.

"Are you all right?" Corey murmured, as much to herself as to Matt as she ran her eyes over his body looking for broken bones. "Why in the world did you lock the door?" she snapped, worry making her angry. As her eyes raked over his body checking for obvious damage, she couldn't help but notice Matt's absolutely incredible looks.

"What happened?" Corey asked as she ran her hands down his arms, and then the one leg that wasn't already injured. Her eyes trailed the line of her hands, checking for signs of blood. She saw how the thick black hair on his chest narrowed to a slight arrow at the waist, and followed it all the way down this time, to a thatch of dark hair that was the perfect frame for his masculinity. His legs were slightly dusted with curly hair, too, and a thin white stripe refocused her attention on his loins, declaring that Matt was not modest when it came to swimwear. As her hands efficiently probed his stomach, checking to see that nothing was ruptured, she glanced up, seeking signs of pain in his flushed face.

Her own face grew heated as she noted that Matt was also aware of the intimacy of their situation. In fact, it was no longer possible for either of them to ignore his rising interest in the feel of her hands on his body. Reaching up, Corey grabbed a towel from the rack and threw it over his lower body, disguising but not hiding his reaction to her.

"What happened? You aren't entirely out of it, if you are able to react like that. If I kicked in that door for nothing, I'll personally see to it that the next moan you make will be for real."

"Corey . . ." Matt finally wheezed. "It's no joke. I was taking a shower, and I slipped. I must have fallen and hit my head. I didn't hear you calling me. The first I recall, you were leaning over me, touching me. . . . I'm sorry if I embarrassed you."

"I shouldn't have said that. I really didn't think you did this on purpose. You're not embarrassing me, it's just a normal physiological reaction." Quickly she asked, "How's your head?" while moving so that she could gently cradle his head in her lap, now running her trained fingers over his skull. She looked into his eyes briefly, checking his pupils. When she saw they looked approximately the same, she sighed in relief.

"You seem fine, but you can never tell with head injuries. Can you stand up?" she asked. "I'd like to get you into bed."

"I've wanted to hear you say that for two weeks," Matt managed to joke. "But I never envisioned that these would be the circumstances." He sat up slowly, reassuring Corey that he was fine. "I had the wind knocked out of me, more than anything else. I landed on your rug, so my head didn't get bumped that hard."

Corey reached up and gathered another towel from her rack and gently dried his body. She looked directly at his shoulder as she ran the towel down his body, unable to follow her eyes and or meet his knowing ones. By the time Corey finished drying him, her face was flushed and her pulse throbbed in her neck. Helping Matt stand was even more difficult as his towel fell to the floor and the full glory of his body pressed into her hip.

"Matt . . ." she managed to request in a strangled tone. "Put the towel around yourself, please."

Chuckling, Matt wrapped the towel around his waist and let go of her. "I'm fine, Corey. But I am a little worried about my cast." They both looked down at his leg and groaned in unison. It had remained in the wet shower stall during his accident and the plaster was disintegrating before their very eyes. Corey looked down ruefully, thinking she should have moved the cast at once.

"Now what should we do?" Corey questioned out loud, casting back to her initial training, trying to recall if any of her emergency first-aid classes ever mentioned casts. She knew a lot about bullet wounds, head injuries, emergency procedures, but not casts. She could splint a broken limb but that was the end of her expertise. Falling back on common sense, she grabbed a sheet from her linen closet. With a yardstick that she broke in half, Corey improvised an emergency splint around the rest of the plaster. Then she helped Matt hop into bed, and ordered him to wait.

Matt agreed, amused to see the change in her. She

was all business at the moment, her years of training coming to the fore. As soon as Corey reentered the room, he was subjected to a light shined in his eyes. Despite his worry over his leg, Matt had to smile when she sighed in relief that he was all right; eyes both dilating properly.

"Were you worried about me, Corey?" Matt asked hopefully.

"You're my responsibility," Corey replied blandly, unwilling to admit that she had been petrified when she first found him on the floor. Her feelings for him were deeper than she wanted to admit. Corey realized how much the man had come to mean to her in that split second when she thought he might be dead or seriously injured. Their time was half over and she realized that she didn't want to lose him. Her very first thought, after she found he was alive, was a crazy hope that he'd be able to stay with her. She didn't want him to go to a hospital. When she had touched his body, her hands lingered, wanting to do more than touch. It had taken every ounce of her professional concentration to force her hands to remain steady, her touch impersonal.

When Corey realized what was uppermost in her mind, she struggled to subdue her emotions. Never in her life had she entertained such an erotic need. She was feeling things that she had arrogantly denied ever existed. With her two previous lovers, sex had been no more than pleasant. Nothing had ever come close to touching the wanton core that Matt seemed capable of arousing.

Finally, her professional persona regained control and her mind cordoned off her erotic thoughts. Corey welcomed the return of her discipline as she covered Matt up with barely a second glance. "I'll be back to check you in a few minutes. Keep your leg still while I call Parker and see what to do about the cast. Are you sure you're in no pain?''

''Absolutely. The back of my head is a trifle sore, but I don't even have a headache. The only part of me that is throbbing,'' Matt told her with a pained grin, ''can't be cured by any pill.''

Corey didn't even dignify that with an answer as she left the room looking remote and cool. Matt wondered what happened. In the bathroom he swore that she was as aroused as he, but somewhere in the past few minutes, Corey had turned her feelings off. Now Matt was getting a glimpse of Corey the agent, the woman who'd successfully coped with stress and fear for years, hiding her emotions from everyone, herself included.

Hopefully it was a reaction to her feelings, and only temporary. Otherwise, Matt feared that he was back to square one with her and he didn't know if there would be time enough to break through again. He was only too aware of the two remaining weeks of his agreed-upon month with Corey. Not that Matt ever entertained any notion of leaving in the contracted time, not after the first day that they'd met. Nonetheless, he wanted Corey in a receptive mood when he told her he wouldn't be leaving on schedule. They might part one day, but not soon. Not soon at all, Matt promised himself as he drifted into a light sleep.

FIVE

Matt awoke an hour later as Corey pried open his eyelids and flashed her light in them. His large hand captured her smaller one and he asked her if everything was all right, letting his mouth drift over her captive wrist and brush the delicate veins there. "Don't pull away, Corey," he whispered softly, "I need you. Hold me, just hold me for a minute."

If he said he wanted her, she would have moved away. If he said that it was only natural, if he said anything else, she would have pulled away. But *need*, that she could understand. Because she found she needed him, too, whether she wanted to or not. So, for a second, she relaxed and let her body guide her mind. Following his gentle pressure on her wrist, Corey slowly lowered her body to the bed, molding her length against his. She let her lips slip over his high cheekbones and touch the lobe of his ear. And when his arms captured hers, she reached out to put her arms around his lean waist, running her palms up his warm back, feeling the muscles contract under her touch. As Matt's tongue reached out for hers, as he insinuated her bottom lip between his, Corey flamed and melted.

Greedily, she imitated his actions, anxious to taste and feel and experience on her own, wanting to forget everything in the rush of fire that roared through her veins. She lost herself in his kiss, in the touch of his hands on her flesh, in the heat that blazed between them.

The center of her body began sending messages to her brain that demanded immediate action. As she shifted to accommodate their need, Corey's leg accidentally brushed the wet sheet that surrounded Matt's leg, activating her defense system. Like a woman drowning, she surfaced from their passion, pulling her lips from his, almost gasping in the shock of separation. "What am I doing?" she asked, more to herself than to him.

"Corey . . ." Matt murmured, reaching up his hand to pull her back to him. "Let me love you."

Hearing those words only reinforced Corey's determination, and she pulled herself the rest of the way off the bed. She stood before Matt, panting but in control. Barely in control, but that was her business. Truthfully, she knew that if they ever reached that same point again, she would not be able to stop. Only the knowledge that Matt had been injured and that they needed to be at a doctor's that very afternoon had kept her from total surrender.

"I called Parker, Matt," Corey announced, fighting to control her breathing and sound professional. Anger simmered in her blue eyes, but Corey refused to acknowledge it aloud. The anger she felt was tinged with fear, and the majority of it was focused on herself. It was not Matt's behavior that was at fault. It was her own. It was not his ardor that frightened her, but her own. "We've got an appointment with a Dr. Murray in three hours. In Boston. He'll have your X-rays and records.''

When Matt asked why they were going to Boston, Corey snapped. "Apparently, you did a bit more damage to your leg than you told me before, and you need an expert to make sure the bones are mending properly. Hopefully he won't have to break all the bones and start over again. I've heard of that happening when the bones didn't align themselves quite properly.'' She took a certain satisfaction when she saw a flicker of concern ripple over his face. "We don't want you to have a permanent limp, do we?'' Corey asked in that patronizing professional tone of voice that doctors and nurses so often employ when they are calmly talking about the things they plan to do to your body. "While you're there, he can check out your head as well.''

"Because I want you and you want me? There's nothing wrong with the way we feel, Corey.''

Ignoring his comment, she moved toward him. "Now, we need to get you up and dressed.'' When he didn't reply right away, Corey asked, "Do you need some help with your clothes?'' praying that he'd say no.

She should have known better, Corey told herself seconds later. He immediately tried to stand up, totally naked since the towel had long ago worked its way loose among the sheets. He'd taken one step when Corey ordered him to sit down. "Hold it, mister. I'll get your cane and your clothes and we'll be on our way. Are you sure you can make it? No pain?''

"I'm fine. My leg feels a bit strange, that's all.''

Corey didn't reply but moved into action. She

found a navy-blue stretch suit that was soft enough to double for pajamas, if needed, and brought them to the bed along with a pair of brief navy underwear. She knelt at his feet to slip the underpants over his cast, now awkward and bulky with a sheet wrapped around it. She averted her eyes while he struggled to stand and pulled the briefs over his still-aroused body. She nearly bit a hole in her cheek in order to divert her attention when she helped him pull up the jogging pants.

After he was decently attired, she walked into the other room, found his cane, and picked up his disk pack. On the off chance that he might have to stay overnight in Boston, she grabbed a spare pair of his jeans and a cranberry sweater to throw in the car. Luckily, she'd had the foresight to change her clothing while Matt rested and was wearing a multilayered outfit of teal blue that could be rearranged for another day's wear if need be. With that possibility in mind, Corey threw the necessities of an overnight stay in her cavernous leather purse. Over the years she learned she could do without most anything if she had her toothbrush and paste, deodorant, and clean underwear.

Getting downstairs was a slow process, with Matt leaning heavily on Corey and his cane. "Are you sure this doesn't hurt?"

"No, but the cast feels odd. Every time I put any weight on it, it sort of slides around. To be honest, I don't want to put any weight on it at all. The doctors in Israel were pretty nasty when they told me what would happen if I didn't follow their orders. A limp was one of the nicer possibilities they mentioned."

Corey didn't say anything more as she eased him into a chair near the back door. She rushed down to her safe, depositing the computer disks of his manuscript and grabbing the .38 Special that she kept for emergencies. It was loaded and ready to go. She then ran a quick check to make sure all the alarms were turned on. As a final touch, she stuck a handwritten note in the door that said she was attending an auction. No one would think twice about that.

Matt dozed off as they skimmed through the barren countryside. Corey ran through little villages, returning to the main road only when a shortcut appreciably decreased the expected travel time. When they reached the outskirts of Boston she was convinced that they had not been followed. She was also blindingly grateful that she was able to slip back into her professional role with such ease. She would deal with all of her unexpected feelings after it was over. When she was safely back in her store. Alone.

Corey was totally alert after the car crossed the Fort Point Channel and was in Boston proper. She was not taking any chances. Her first destination was a large parking facility near a group of state and federal buildings that were centered near the middle of the city. She chose a parking structure that allowed you to drive your own car up and parked her car near the top, right next to the elevator. There she awoke Matt, gently shaking his shoulder. "We're in Boston, Matt. You need to wake up."

"Where are we?" he asked, rubbing his fist across his eyes like a little boy. He hadn't intended to go to sleep, but the gentle motion of the car had induced him into a light slumber. Surprisingly, he felt better, much refreshed. "I can't believe I went to sleep again."

"We're in a parking garage just off Haymarket Square."

"Is my doctor in there?" Matt asked, puzzled,

recalling vaguely that government offices were traditionally associated with this area, not medical facilities.

"No, he's several blocks away, near Boston General."

"Why are we here?"

"A few basic precautions. I'm sure we are still clean, so I'm going to ditch my car and we'll take a taxi from here on. I have my own plates on this car and it could be traced back if anyone spots you."

"Okay."

"Can you walk?" Corey asked with an edge in her voice.

"For a while. Lead on. It should be interesting to see you in action," he told her, trying to deny his growing feeling of unease. He'd ignored the danger for the last couple of weeks, tucked safely away in Corey's refuge. Now the real world was intruding again, and Matt felt himself grow cold.

Corey gave him a quick stare. "Stop joking. This is not a game," She told him in a quiet voice.

Subdued by his memories and the realization that Corey was dead serious, Matt followed Corey's directions. Even if she thought he'd been kidding, Matt had not. He was interested to see the agent Corey, in order to compare her with the real live woman, the one who'd melted in his arms not more than a few hours ago. It would be interesting, if only he didn't have to think of the reason they were being so painfully careful.

Corey motioned Matt to join her as they exited from the elevator onto the main floor of the garage. Immediately, she turned and whispered for him to lean back against the wall, pretending to wait for someone while she found them their next ride. Instead of walking out to the street to hail a cab, she walked over to the young man who ran the garage. She had spotted a For Sale sign in a car that most likely belonged to the parking attendant. It was a beat-up Toyota sedan, several years old, rusted through in places and quite dented from city driving. Corey walked over to the young man and held a whispered conversation with him for several minutes. As Matt was beginning to get annoyed, Corey broke away from the boy, walked over to the Toyota, and drove up to him.

"Get in," she ordered. "I rented us a car." With a brilliant smile, she thanked the boy and told him they'd be back by seven.

"What did you do, Corey?"

"Offered him seventy-five dollars to rent his car for one day."

"It's not worth it. A new Caddy doesn't rent for much more than that."

"I know, but this way we have our own car, and no way to be traced. No records, no paperwork."

"What did you tell that kid?"

"That we're married lovers. A private detective is following us and we wanted to spend the day together."

Matt tried to control his reaction but wasn't able to. Soon he was chuckling out loud and forced Corey to ask him what he found so funny. "I don't know. I just never imagined myself in this situation. A private detective is following us? Pretty soon I expect someone to shout Candid Camera over my shoulder."

"It's all right, Matt," Corey said soothingly. "I understand how you feel. Actually, humor is one of the better ways of dealing with fear."

Matt sat quietly as they drove through the streets. She was right. He was scared. His broken leg was real and so were the terrorists who had killed his wife and son so long ago, starting this complicated trail. Somehow in the past couple of weeks, he had pushed all of that to the back of his mind. He'd reduced the terrorists to paper figures, becoming involved in the financial picture, tracing the impartial money and ignoring the reality of their existence. Hidden in Corey's warm house, it seemed as though the PF and the cruelty of their lives existed in another dimension. But in four short hours, his little fantasy world was gone and reality was back. This was real, the danger was real, and suddenly Matt found himself wondering how real Corey was. Had his intimacy with her been just another illusion? Was his fascination with her and her problems another way of denying his own guilt?

Corey finally broke the silence by asking how he felt, wondering just what he was thinking. She knew that her old life hadn't seemed real to him, not until now. It *was* real, however, and the sooner he saw her as she truly was, the better. She was no tragic heroine from a fairy-tale past. She was a woman who had worked in a tense, frightening profession for years, one who finally made a mistake that was unforgivable. Once he knew what she'd done, he'd despise her. Even if he understood her motives, there was no way to dismiss what had happened.

Forcing her mind back to the present, Corey pulled into yet another parking structure. This one belonged to the doctor's combination building and parking structure where they were headed. It was an unusual setup, the floor-by-floor parking connected directly to the doctor's office building so that one could enter the doctor's offices on each floor directly from the parking area.

When she was asked by the guard on duty which doctor she planned on seeing, she lied and played her flighty female role. "Maybe you can help me," she said to the older man, fluttering her eyelashes. "I made an appointment with my girlfriend's . . . female doctor, you know what I mean," she said, turning her eyes down. "And I've forgotten his name. Are there any of those kinds of doctors in this building? I do think this is the right place." When the man obligingly told her the name of several gynecologists, she picked one at random and thanked him sweetly. He told her that Dr. Raymond's offices were on the fourth level and she drove off with a casual wave.

"That was clever, but sickening," Matt snorted from the backseat.

"You'd be surprised at how stupid men are willing to think women are. It's totally amazing. But it got us in without revealing the name of your doctor, didn't it?"

Matt had to agree that it had worked and watched Corey drive expertly to the eighth floor, again parking nose-out, equidistant from the elevator and stairs.

"How do you know what floor my doctor is on?" Matt questioned.

"Parker told me. He's on six. And yes, I know that this is eight. We'll park up here, just in case. There's usually an elevator in these places. You won't have any farther to walk. Come, let's go," Corey urged him, holding his elbow while she cradled her gun within her shoulder bag on the other hip. "Remember, no names used in the doctor's office."

Two hours later, Matt walked up to her, favoring his leg but walking with no noticeable limp. "I'm fine," Matt grinned. "I can do anything with my leg

I used to do, only a bit more slowly for the next couple of weeks." With a smile belying the relief he felt, Matt told her that his leg was weak but fine. "No permanent damage was done. All I need is to exercise it and take it slow for a couple of weeks." Taking her into his arms, he pretended to dance with her right there in the hall of the doctor's examining wing. "Want to help me exercise?" Matt asked, pressing his body tight against hers.

"What's gotten into you?" Corey asked, wondering if the same man walked out of the office who had walked in. "Did that doctor give you a shot of something?"

"No, it's just that my leg is all right! It's fine, all back to normal. No limp. No permanent damage, no nothing," Matt announced, unable to hide the relief. "I feel like celebrating. Let's get some champagne on the way home."

"We'll see," Corey hedged. From the exuberance of his reaction it was obvious that Matt had been more than a bit worried about his leg. That relief added to his reaction to the danger, and her taking charge probably triggered his desire to conquer her sexually. At least Corey told herself that explained his reaction and allowed her to totally ignore their unfinished business from earlier that morning.

As Corey glanced casually through the glass in the nurses' station out into the waiting room, her cheerful expression vanished. Two very large men, dark-haired, dark-complected, both impeccably dressed in somber suits stood near the doorway. They were menacingly out of place in the doctor's waiting room; both displayed the unmistakable bulges in their jackets that signaled concealed guns.

"Shut up!" Corey ordered, pulling him back. Smiling, she told the nurse that the doctor needed to see Matt one more time, and turned Matt to retrace his steps. Walking into the doctor's office, she firmly shut the door and cut the older man off in the middle of his question.

"Dr. Murray, I presume you realized that Stone is in danger when Parker briefed you on his injury?" When the startled man nodded his head, Corey continued to speak without interruption, very clearly and very rapidly. "We have a problem. It seems that the men who are after Stone got word that he is here. The 'how' can be dealt with later. Now I need two things from you. One, do not mention anything about this visit to anyone, don't mention me at all—anything that could be used to track us down. Two, slip us out your back door, pretending to your staff that we are still here."

The orthopedist became appreciably paler as Corey spoke, but he plunged into action immediately. "I'm sorry," he said in a loud voice opening his door. "I'm going to have to let you sit here and wait for the last X-ray to be developed," he said, waving them through a door in his office that opened to the corridor. "I'm sorry for any inconvenience," he said, his eyes reflecting his apology.

"Not your fault," Corey said, giving the man a small wave. "Now, Matt . . ." Corey ordered briskly as soon as the door was shut, "don't look around and go down to the other end of the hall." There she cursed as the fire door remained locked and pulled a small pick from her purse. Within seconds the door was open and then silently closed behind them. "Now, climb. I'm sorry we can't risk the elevator."

"I'll be fine," Matt insisted as he climbed as fast as his weakened leg permitted. After checking the eighth-floor corridor to make sure that it was clear, they made their way back to the Toyota. Corey sighed in relief when she saw that there was no one near it. She forced Matt to lie on the floor in the backseat and told him that she planned to drive down, hope-fully unnoticed.

Corey spoke firmly as she opened the front door of the small sedan and got into the driver's seat. "I want you to follow my instructions now, without question. I'll explain everything later. Is that all right?"

"I trust you, Corey," Matt said in a steady voice, hunching down. "Don't worry about me."

Even as concerned as she was, Corey couldn't help feel a deep shaft of warmth enter her when she heard his words. She swore she would keep him safe. For the first time in a year, Corey was grateful for her past, grateful for the skills she hoped would keep him alive. Nothing else mattered.

Putting on her seat belt, Corey ordered Matt to brace himself as she took off down the ramp. She had her .38 hidden in the pocket of her jacket, and wasn't sure what to expect from the sixth floor. She slowed but did not stop when another large gunman stood in the center of the down ramp, motioning her to stop. Instead, she floored the car, abruptly turned, and continued to descend, going the wrong way on the up ramp. The man turned and ran after her, but Corey was gone before he could fire his weapon. Luck was with them and they reached the street without any further resistance.

Corey traveled a few blocks until she was sure that she hadn't been followed. Then she drove to the Boston Common, stopping at one of the phone booths that were placed so the driver could call from his car. As she dialed Parker's number, she asked Matt to think of what information he had given the doctor during their conversation. She particularly asked him if either her name, the name of the antique shop, or the town they were in on the Cape were mentioned. After Matt replied negatively to all three questions, Corey remained silent until he finally asked her what would happen to them now.

"Once Parker catches the men watching for you and finds out how they found you, we can probably go back home."

Matt smiled at the way Corey had said "we can go home" and hoped that she was including him in her definition. During the past two weeks, home had changed its definition for him. Home was no longer a place, but a person, a tall blond woman who was still unwilling to admit that she belonged with him.

"That's all we can do for now," Corey told Matt a few minutes later as she pulled away from the phone. "We're checking into a hotel for the night. I'm sure the man who chased us in the parking ramp has the license plate and will be able to trace this car in a short time. The agency'll have people over to the parking lot and the parking attendant's home as soon as possible. They should be able to pick up some of the men there and find out exactly what we're dealing with. We need to dump this car at the Market Square and rent ourselves another."

"Will the boy get hurt?" Matt asked from the backseat.

"He shouldn't. Parker's men should be with him within minutes and probably move him to a safer location until they round up those goons after us. It'll take those thugs at least an hour to trace the license number and then find the garage where the kid works. By the time they show up, our guys will be waiting for them. I'm betting that boy will find this all a big adventure, a story to tell his grandchildren some-day.'' Corey crossed her fingers as she said that, knowing that there was a chance that the boy would be injured—if everyone didn't do their jobs right. She should never have involved him, Corey berated herself. Taking a deep breath, she ordered herself to stop borrowing trouble. The boy would be fine.

"One of Parker's men is moving my car from the garage right now. He'll leave it at an arranged hotel for us so we'll be back to square one in another hour," Corey explained. "We should be clear as soon as the men are picked up. Then we can go back to the Cape.''

An hour later, Matt was riding in yet another strange car. He was sitting beside a woman who was suddenly very tense. She had abruptly decided to rent another car, this time from Hertz, as a precaution, and they'd driven around for at least another half hour before she trusted herself to register at a small motel near Boston University.

As they drove around to the room, Matt glanced over the parking lot, searching for their blue Chevy but not finding it. When Matt asked Corey where it was, she told him, "Don't worry, I know it's not here. This isn't the motel where Parker expects us to stay.'' When she caught sight of his raised eyebrow, she turned to him. "I'm not taking any chances with you,'' she announced in a neutral voice. "After I made those arrangements with Parker, I saw some-thing I didn't like. A car might have been following us. Probably it was a coincidence, but I'm not taking even the slightest chance that there's a leak somewhere in Parker's camp, or at the local Boston office. Parker will know exactly how and why those two men showed up in the doctor's office. I'll check in with him in the morning. Until then we are totally incommunicado.''

SIX

"How do you suppose they found us?" Matt finally asked, more interested in breaking the tension-filled silence than in the answer to his question. He had been staring at Corey and Corey had been staring at the walls, at the bed, at anything but him for the last half hour. Matt had to do something before he stalked over to Corey and shook her. It was sheer torture sitting on the motel bed pretending to be nonchalant.

He had expected to relax once he and Corey had checked into the room, but it hadn't happened that way. Instead of leaning back in relief, Corey had become more nervous. Each passing minute added to the invisible tension as Corey sat in a chair by the curtained window, paused in readiness to escape. Finally Matt had broken the silence, asking what he hoped she would consider a pertinent question. As he watched, Corey turned slowly in his direction, finally focusing on the lamp near his head.

"The doctor's office is the most likely possibility," Corey speculated in a remote voice. "Someone on the doctor's staff probably took a bribe. It's possible that they targeted the top orthopedists all along the East Coast. If they didn't bribe somebody in the office, they might have placed a man in the major medical buildings where you might show up. Maybe the guard who told us the floor numbers.''

Restlessly, Corey stood up and walked two paces to the curtained window before she went on. "The only fact they had to work with was your broken leg. Sooner or later, you were bound to surface to have it checked by an expert. They obviously have no problem with either money or manpower, so it was just a matter of organizing the stakeout. There can't be more than three or four top medical groups that would suit you here in Boston. Probably fewer in most of the smaller cities.''

After a brief pause, Corey went on in her careful voice, "I really don't think there is a leak in Washington, or they'd have been out to the Cape long ago. Still, until Parker's absolutely sure, we'll wait here.''

"You're good at this.''

"I *was* good, past tense. I should have noticed those thugs before we almost walked into them.''

"There was no way you could have known. As soon as you saw them, you got us out of there. You handled the situation perfectly. I have no doubts about your ability, Corey, I never did.'' Thinking out loud, Matt added, "If anything, you were too good, weren't you?''

"What do you mean? No one can be too good, it's like being too thin or too rich—you can't ever be too good an agent,'' Corey stated categorically.

"I meant that it was your entire life, that you took it too seriously,'' Matt said softly, hoping that she might be able to talk now. She was strung tighter than a wire and she needed to release some of her tension. He found himself wondering if she was always like this after an assignment, or was it his presence?

"Of course it was my whole life. What do you expect? That I'd turn off my bugs, close up shop and say, 'hey, guys, it's my night off. Let's go bowling, grab a burger, go back into the straight world?' "

"No, I meant that you never realized that you could turn it off, at least between assignments. Did you ever really separate yourself from your job?"

"Well, I turned it off all right—permanently. Or I will as soon as you're safe and the book's done."

"Why did you quit, Corey? Will you tell me now?"

"I told you before, it's none of your business. Just be glad that I remembered enough to get us out of the way today."

"I am. I only hope it didn't bring back too many memories." When Corey shrugged, he went on. "Is that what's bothering you now? Did the excitement of it all get to you? Are you sorry that you're quitting?"

"Give me a break, Herr Doktor," Corey snapped, smarting under his probing questions. She didn't need to be analyzed, she just needed to get out of this room and away from him. "For the last time, I'm not sorry I'm quitting. I'm not dredging up old memories. I'm fine, perfectly fine."

"Sure, you're just great, Madam Agent. Give me some credit, Corey," Matt snapped back. "I've gotten to know you pretty well over the last two weeks, and something is driving you crazy. So what is it? Either you're wanting to get back into the old life or the memories of your old life are bothering you? It's got to be one or the other, lady." When Corey turned to glare at him, he shrugged his shoulders in an imitation of her previous movement. "All right, have it your way. Everything's just perfect. Then tell me, can we go home in the morning?"

"I hope so. As soon as Parker cleans up this little group and finds out what they know, we can drive back to the Cape without company. Then you can have your last two weeks and finish your book."

"I'm not sure I can be finished in two weeks," Matt replied without thinking. This was not the time to tell her that, Matt immediately swore at himself, but it was too late to take back the words now. Holding his breath, he added, "I might need more time."

"You have to be done. You promised."

"Are you going to make me leave if my book isn't finished?"

"No," Corey admitted slowly, honesty prevailing over her need for self-protection. "You know that I wouldn't do that."

"Then why are you so anxious for me to leave?"

"I'm not," Corey denied, unconsciously fiddling with the strings to the window curtain. "I want you safe, that's all. The sooner the book is finished, the sooner you'll be out of danger." Before Matt had a chance to interrupt her again, she quickly asked him if he was hungry. "I'll go and find us something," she offered.

"What about room service? Wouldn't that be easier?" Matt asked with a trace of a smile. He was beginning to think—or hope—that he understood what was making Corey so jumpy. There might be a third explanation to her nervousness, one that had to do only with him and their passionate encounter only hours ago. Foolishly, Matt let himself hope. She hadn't looked directly at him since they entered the room, her restless eyes flitting anywhere but near him. "I'm sorry I slipped and caused all this mess."

"It certainly wasn't your fault. Anyone can slip in the shower, especially if they're wearing a cast on one leg," Corey said hoarsely. "In the long run, it probably doesn't matter," she told him, clearing her throat. "We would have had the same problem when we came in to get your cast off anyway."

Matt caught Corey unawares with his next question, pulling her into a maelstrom of emotions. "How do you usually work off all this energy?" he asked in a low growl, intentionally giving his question a sexual overtone. He had to know if that was what was causing Corey's nervousness. "You must still be pretty high on adrenaline. I know I am. Perhaps you should be lying down next to me," he offered, patting the bed beside him.

His questions evoked memories of other places, other assignments, other men who'd made similar suggestions. Memories of fear, the coppery taste of blood from lips that were bitten through. She'd seldom felt anything but relief when the danger was over—knee-shaking weakness that she had managed to hide most of the time. If Matt only knew how very unglamorous her life had been, he'd laugh. She hadn't gotten high on the danger, she hadn't enjoyed the feeling of living on the edge. Her job had been frightening and fascinating, never erotic. The only man she'd loved in her years as an agent had been in her last year in the Mideast, and the memories of that so-called love were tinged with fear, hatred, and a deep guilt.

"Are you asking me to s-sleep with you? You've watched too many spy movies. We're together in here tonight because I need to protect you, no other reason." Stalking to the dresser, she opened a drawer and tossed the room service menu at Matt. "Choose what you want and I'll call in the order. I'll be back in a second," she told him, stepping out the door. "I've got to check out the car."

"Corey . . ." Matt called to her before the door closed, "I wondered if you wanted me to rub your back, that's all." He didn't want her to think that he'd really meant what he'd implied. That crack had been a deliberate one, designed solely to get a response out of her. It had done that, all right, Matt told himself ruefully—she had responded by moving right out of the room. Sitting back, Matt wondered exactly what was going on inside Corey's lovely head and how he could find out.

Corey paused a moment to check the lock before she walked away from the room. She didn't need to check out the car, she needed to get away from Matt. Away from the feeling he elicited in her. Never had she wanted a man like she wanted him. If he so much as touched her, she knew she'd surrender. Surrender everything—her self-respect, her professionalism, and, even worse, her heart. Somehow Corey had to bring her emotions back under control. She needed to protect Matt. Even more difficult, she had to stay away from him.

Corey walked once around the parking lot briskly and then a second time more slowly before finally coming to a rest beneath a tall oak tree directly across the parking lot from the room. The best idea she'd had so far was staying out here, standing guard all night.

All of her good intentions were crumbling. When she'd seen Matt that morning, naked and vulnerable, she realized that she wanted him, in a way that she never had wanted any other man. In a way she'd never imagined a woman could want a man. Corey's dilemma was that while she could no longer deny her need, neither could she ever give in to it. Nothing but pain would follow. She wasn't right for Matt. They could have nothing more than a brief affair.

Memories of her last assignment and its tragic end ran through her mind. Memories of the last man she'd loved—her supervisor Chuck Durent. Why, she asked herself for the millionth time, had she trusted him? Why hadn't she followed her instincts and gone over his head before it was too late? If she had listened to her own feelings, if she had used her intelligence, if she hadn't followed orders, nineteen innocent people might still be alive.

That day would be forever imprinted in her mind. It had been late morning when she first heard the most recent tape from the elaborate series of listening devices that she'd planted, with great difficulty, in a secret meeting place of the PF. A splinter group was planning to hijack an Israeli bus the next morning.

Corey expected Chuck to be excited by the tangible results and to immediately notify the Israelis. Instead, he'd thanked her for the information and ordered her to go back to work. When Corey asked, he'd assured her that he was taking proper precautions and invoked his official authority to order her to keep the information confidential. Corey had complied but wondered why he'd felt obliged to be so formal. After all, they were engaged.

At dinner that evening, Corey again asked what

happened. Chuck tried to ignore her, but when Corey insisted, he told her the information wasn't reliable enough to pass on. They'd argued for hours, over one long, hot, never-to-be-forgotten night. Finally Chuck shouted the truth at her. He hadn't told anyone of the plan because he wanted to keep his listening post intact. The takeover of a bus wasn't "major" enough. He ignored it rather than lose his chance for something "better," something newsworthy enough to earn a promotion.

Most of the time, Corey was successful in repressing the rest of her memory of the remainder of her last night as an agent. But not tonight. Tonight she remembered how Chuck had taken her, how his body possessed hers against her will, using his strength to subjugate her, both mentally and physically.

The next morning it was all over. The PF had hijacked the bus. The deal had soured and nineteen innocent people had been killed. Chuck expected Corey to keep her mouth shut, once it was too late. He had expected her total loyalty since they were engaged, insisting that if she loved him, she would do whatever he said. He'd even hinted she had to stay quiet for the sake of her own career.

Corey called Parker as soon as she'd been able, telling him everything but the most intimate details of her last night with Chuck. Then she'd rushed to the building the terrorists occupied, planning on confiscating all of the tapes. One of the PF members saw her leaving and shot her. Only a quick response by a passing soldier saved her life.

Once she left the hospital, she'd sent Parker a letter of resignation. As she lay recovering, Corey realized that she had to quit. The incident with Chuck was the last straw, but not, Corey finally admitted, the entire reason that she quit. Ten years of service were enough. She had nothing left to give. She was finished with fear and death and lies. Finished until the day Matt arrived at her back door and made Corey remember.

She stood for a long while, leaning against the tree, letting the bark press against her tender skin. If Matt could only see the scars that didn't show, he wouldn't want her. Eventually she walked back, calm and empty.

Matt was silent as she entered the room, watching her with intense eyes. "Are you all right?" he finally inquired, his voice muted as though in a waiting room. Somewhere in the darkness, Corey had come to terms with whatever was bothering her. Corey the agent, not Corey the woman had come back. "When you didn't come back in half an hour, I ordered us dinner and it should be here soon."

"Good," Corey acknowledged as she eased off the unlined jacket and hung it on a hanger. "How is your leg?"

"Fine," he told her as a knock sounded at the door and Corey turned to tuck her gun in the pocket of her wool slacks. She motioned Matt to move into the bathroom and then she answered the door. Handing the boy a five-dollar bill, she signed the meal slip and told him to leave the table. "I'll serve it myself."

They ate in a somber silence, making occasional bland comments to each other but never achieving the comfortable camaraderie that they shared back on the Cape. Finally, Corey turned on the television. She needed the mindless chatter of a local newscast to fill her mind. When it was finally late enough, Corey announced that she'd do a final check of the grounds while Matt got into bed, and she again walked out into the cold night.

By the time she returned, Matt was asleep in bed, his clothing neatly folded on a chair next to the television. The light in the bathroom spilled out of the door illuminating his handsome face. Corey was drawn over to stand by his bed to watch him while he slept. His face was relaxed, and a lock of wavy black hair fell haphazardly over his forehead. His beautiful, almost-straight nose was outlined by the light, and his spiky eyelashes cast shadows on his bronzed cheeks. Corey's hand reached down of its own accord and smoothed the silky ebony strands back from his eyes, lingering on the brow that was so smooth and unlined in sleep.

Eventually Corey moved, slipping off her slacks and blouse, content to sleep in her beige silk teddy, with the gun under her pillow. Something awakened her around three in the morning, a low moaning sound that made her spring from her bed to the windows. The parking lot was deserted. Turning, she saw that Matt was in the midst of a dream, thrashing in his sleep. Low sobs and deep groans shook his lean body.

Touching his arm, Corey was struck with the look of suffering on his face, the lone tear escaping from under his clenched lids.

"Matt, Matt, please wake up," she murmured while lightly shaking his shoulder.

"My love," Matt moaned, lifting his arms up around her, pulling her unerringly to his warmth. "I thought I'd lost you. . . . I need you so," Matt whispered against her throat, his tongue busily stroking, fanning the embers that had smoldered for so long. When Corey opened her lips to answer, he claimed them, warm and open and giving, for his own. His hands were feverish on her body, touching her shoulder and running down, down the long length of her and back again, as though he needed to reassure himself of her presence.

"Oh, Matt, this is wrong . . ." she protested, but she couldn't continue as his tongue invaded her mouth and turned her moan into something more, into a pleasurable sound that was swallowed up in the passion that they created together. Corey was lost in urgency, overwhelmed by a frantic need to touch and be touched. Her hands ran down his muscled chest, seeking and finding the small nipples that responded to her touch so strongly.

She arched her back in silent offering when Matt finally left her lips, his mouth moving down her neck into the silken valley that sheltered her throbbing breasts. With a bold move, Matt gripped the silk teddy with his trembling fingers and pulled it down to expose her pearly flesh, firm peaks topped with rosy nipples, turned hard in anticipation.

As Matt's mouth settled over one throbbing peak, he used his tongue and teeth to catapult Corey to heights of need that she had never before glimpsed. Working on instinct alone, Corey ran her hands through his thick black hair, urging him to take more of her, to continue to teach her the ways of desire. As he moved his head from one ruby-hard peak to the other, he murmured, "Oh, Sally," into the valley of her breasts and Corey died a little.

She felt Matt's mouth move over her skin, but the skin was no longer her own. It was someone else's. It was Sally's body that he desired, Sally's love that he needed, Corey screamed in her mind, frozen into immobility in his arms. Abruptly regaining the use of her limbs, she took his hands in her strong ones, slowly loosing his hold on her body.

Matt fully awoke as she gently tried to elude his embrace. His nightmare had turned into an erotic dream and he didn't want to stop dreaming. When he opened his eyes, Corey stood over his bed, mere inches from him. Quickly he took in her disheveled appearance, her kiss-reddened lips, the beige silk teddy that was precariously hanging around her hips.

"What happened?"

"Nothing," Corey finally was able to say, her voice harsh with suppressed feeling. "You were having a dream." When Matt reached for her, she pulled away from him and walked quickly into the bathroom, softly closing the door behind her.

"Damn," Matt said as he sat up in his bed, finding himself still aroused from his encounter. Vaguely he remembered his nightmare and then his dream, where Corey had come to him, offering love and warmth. Then, he remembered with a groan of self-disgust, he'd called her Sally. He stood up and walked to the bathroom door, wanting to do something to make it right.

"Corey, please come out. I can explain everything. It isn't what you think." After several minutes elapsed, he finally announced, "I'm coming in, if you won't come out. I'm going to break in the door if you don't come out. I hope I don't break my blasted leg again." It was not a fair ploy, but he felt it was a necessary one. As Matt prepared to attack the door, he heard a small click and the door swung open.

Looking through him, Corey stood tall and composed. Her hair was still mussed from his loving, but her eyes were cold and distant. She wore only her wrinkled teddy, but a suit of armor would not have been more impenetrable. "Go back to bed. I won't be responsible for injuring your leg. It wouldn't be safe for you to return to Dr. Murray in the morning." With that, she turned to close the door, but Matt was desperate, and he put a foot out to block the door's closing.

"Corey, honey, let me explain."

"There is nothing more to say, nothing to explain." With a flicker of pain escaping for a second from behind her composed features, Corey told him calmly, "It was all my fault. You aren't responsible for your dreams, professor. Now, go back to bed."

Matt stood as she closed the door in his face, for once in his life utterly unable to decide what to do. He was afraid to force the issue any further. She was hurting; he was responsible. It didn't matter that it was an accident, that it was the workings of his subconscious mind in a stressful situation.

Corey stepped into the shower letting the warm water run over her frozen body, trying to remove the taste of Matt's mouth from her own, the feel of his mouth on her body. The shock had worn off and cold reality had seeped into her. Turning off the water, she shook her head and started to dry herself.

It was the surprise that bothered her the most, she decided while she combed her hair and wrapped a large towel around herself. She actually thought she was falling in love with him, and all along he had wanted another woman. It only went to prove, Corey told herself, that she'd made the right decision to leave Parker last year. She could not trust either her instincts or her judgment.

When Corey emerged from the steamy bathroom wrapped in a towel, Matt breathed a sigh of relief. "Let me explain. I know it was unforgivable, but I can explain."

"It really doesn't matter," Corey said matter-of-factly. "It's almost dawn. Why don't you lie down and get a little sleep while I go and check with Parker." She casually grabbed her clothing and walked back to the bathroom, ignoring him as though he were a piece of the furniture.

Cursing himself, Matt acknowledged that his Corey was in deep hiding. This was the professional agent with him now, the woman who had for ten years dealt with suspicion, tension, and death so calmly. At least, Matt told himself as he started to dress, she was still speaking to him.

An hour later they were seated at a small restaurant, reading the breakfast menus as if nothing had happened. Corey mechanically smiled when the waitress asked for their order.

"I'll have two eggs, over easy," Matt decided, "and bacon, toast, and coffee. How about you?"

"The same, please," she agreed, again glancing over the parking lot with restless eyes.

"Corey, speak to me."

"I am speaking to you, Dr. Stone."

"I'm sorry about last night."

"Don't be. It wasn't your fault. It wasn't my fault. It just happened. We're both adults and in a stressful situation. Stranger things have happened. No one was hurt. It's forgotten."

"No, Corey. I won't forget it. You were hurt, and I was hurt. Let me explain who Sally was . . ."

"I know that Sally is your dead wife." Corey had remembered that this morning, after she'd had a chance to think. "That says it all. Don't say another word. I will not talk about this any more or you will get yourself another babysitter. Is that clear?"

"Does that mean we can go back to the Cape and I can finish my book?" Matt asked her after a long pause. He'd been sure that this would be his very last chance with Corey, that she'd dump him onto Parker so fast that he'd be history in an hour. Or worse, that he'd driven her back to Parker, to the life that he knew was wrong for a sensitive woman like her. If he had the time, he could find a way to reach her again.

"I don't see why not. As long as you promise to keep our relationship professional," Corey replied as she sipped her coffee. "I made a deal with Parker over you, and I don't intend to renege on it. I owe you two more weeks, and you'll get them. I would never break my word over such a trivial incident."

"It wasn't trivial to me and I know it wasn't to you, either."

"Grow up, Stone," Corey said. "Weren't you the one who was talking about adrenaline, sex, and spys? It was just one of those things," Corey told him, explaining her behavior to herself as well as to him. "Agents do things like that all the time." It didn't matter that she hadn't been like all the other agents before. She obviously was now.

Matt watched her with hooded eyes, knowing full well that she was lying to him and to herself. Whatever had happened in her past, she was not terribly sophisticated sexually—at least not sexually awakened. That he knew from her reactions to him, to the surprised excitement that she'd shown whenever he touched her. This was not the time, however, to deal with that. For the moment, he was more than relieved to be given a second chance. Turning to his breakfast he motioned Corey to eat. "Did you find out anything about our Middle Eastern friends?" he asked her. "Is it safe to pick up your car and go home?"

"We'll know for sure in another hour or so. They picked up the men we saw in Murray's office. Now they're trying to find out the extent of their operation. Parker is pretty sure that all of the men were detained. We should be fine."

"It was a busy morning, it seems, for all of us," Matt said sardonically, pleased beyond belief when he saw the tiny corner of Corey's lips begin to lift in a smile. She repressed it immediately, of course, but it had been there.

"Did Parker tell you what country they were from? I'm curious as to exactly who is trying to stop my book. It could be any of several leaders who are pretending to maintain good relations with the West while secretly backing the terrorist groups."

"I'll find out what passports they had, although you know that isn't usually much of a clue."

"That's for sure. I've had three different kinds myself."

"How did you manage that?" Corey asked, drawn into conversation, regardless of her vows to ignore him at all costs.

"Nothing too fancy. I have my own US one, and the Israelis gave me one to help get me back here to Parker."

"You said you had three. What was the third?"

"Lebanese. I bought it in Beirut."

"Why did you do that?"

"There were some people I needed to interview.

The only way I could get to them required phony ID.''

''Your book must be very important to you, if you risked your life for it. I never asked why you were writing it in the first place. Most professors don't do their research in war zones.''

''It's an important book. It tells a story that has to be told. I have personal reasons, for writing it, ones I suspect very much like yours for retiring.'' When Corey looked up at him sharply, denial on her lips, Matt went on. ''Remember the night that we talked, and you promised to edit it?''

Corey nodded her head reluctantly. That night was one of her best memories, and she didn't want it tainted by what had happened last night. Silently she thought about Matt, and slowly some of the ice that had frozen around her heart melted. It really hadn't been his fault. Nothing had really happened. They shared a few kisses, she'd given him a bit of solace from a nightmare. That was all. They could remain friends, Corey thought. It surprised her how very intensely she wanted that.

Matt sat, watching the emotions glide over Corey's face, afraid to break her train of thought. She was back, the woman he wanted. Her face was once again alive with feelings. For a brief, unguarded moment, moods flowed across her face. He saw her hurt, her puzzlement, and thankfully saw the moment that she decided to give him another chance.

''Will you still help me? This book is going to make a difference, it has to. It doesn't really matter why I'm writing it, only that the information has to get out. Bits of your actual experience should really spice it up. Maybe we could turn it into a best-seller. The more people who read it, the better. The only way things will change is for the public to find out what's really happening.''

"Okay, professor," Corey told him, doubting her sanity. She could keep their relationship friendly now that she knew he was still in love with his lost wife.

Matt sat back, contented for the moment. He would have his chance to explain about the book and Sally. He would make his chance to win her back. And win her he would, for this incident made him realize just what was going on. He had fallen in love with Corey, fallen in love for the second time in his life. Corey was his, whether she realized it or not.

SEVEN

After breakfast, Corey drove around for nearly a half hour until she was certain they weren't being followed. Only then did she stop at a self-service gas station and dial Parker's familiar number for the second time within three hours.

"Why did you go off on your own last night?" Parker asked with deceptive calm. "And don't hang up on me like you did this morning. It's not good for my blood pressure." Parker was referring to the brief call he'd gotten from Corey earlier that day. She asked him if the terrorists had been captured. When told they'd been in custody for less than an hour, she'd hung up.

"I thought we'd be safer on our own. How did they find Matt? Have you convinced them to talk yet?"

"You were right about everything, Corey. Money was no object in this operation. They offered fifty thousand dollars, cash, no questions asked, for calling a number if a man fitting Matt's description showed up. It was the receptionist in Murray's office. We traced the number we got from her to a house they'd rented in Boston. We picked up several men there and two more at the garage attendant's place. Unfortunately, one of your would-be assailants was slightly injured during his arrest and we had to treat him. Since he required a shot of sodium pentothal when they stitched up his arm, he talked freely. We have the entire bunch of them detained. At least until we can sort out who has diplomatic immunity and who doesn't. You know how long that can take. . . . In the meantime, I'm almost positive you're clear. You are a mystery woman as far as they're concerned. The way you handled the car leaves you perfectly anonymous. Good work.''

"Thanks," Corey said, and then waited.

"I wish you'd come back to us," Parker said into the long silence, finally mentioning her past, "even if only to the lab. I've told you before that thing with Chuck was a fluke. He was totally out of line. No matter what happened, though, you were not responsible. It was just an extremely unfortunate incident.''

"I know," Corey admitted for the first time. "That doesn't matter. Chuck's behavior was never the real problem. It was *my* behavior that was. *My* judgment that was off. Mine! And quit mentioning the lab. I'm not stupid. I know exactly what would happen. First the lab, then it'd be 'Just supervise this one little job.' Then 'Just *do* this one little job.' Then boom, I'd be right where I started." Suddenly fed up with it all, Corey snapped, "No more! I'm out. Gone. As soon as Stone finishes his lousy book. So tell me, officially, can we go back? I want him to write as fast as he can and get all of you out of my life.''

Parker smiled, encouraged by her fiery reaction. Whatever had happened, Corey was beginning to sound like herself again. For too many months she

had been so cool and reserved that he'd almost forgotten her feisty spirit and stubborn self-confidence.
Stone must be getting to her, or else the emotional
excitement that comes from the chase. Parker hoped
it was the job she was missing, but if not, he was at
least pleased that she was coming out of her icy
cocoon. Perhaps she'd at least run a safe house for
him now and again or send him an occasional electronic toy. Nothing bothered Parker more than the
waste of a good agent.

"Go back. I put two men at the hotel four blocks
from you in case of emergency. So far they've seen
nothing unusual. Call me if you have any trouble
getting out of Boston."

"We're clear," Corey announced as she walked
back to the car. "We'll swing by, pick up my car,
and be on our way back within the hour. How's your
leg this morning?"

"Fine, all things considered. It still feels kinda
weak," Matt said, exaggerating the condition of his
leg slightly. He only had two weeks to break through
to her. That wasn't long, and he needed every little
edge to thaw her reserve and rekindle the fire they'd
toyed with earlier that morning. He sighed loudly,
thinking that a little sympathy couldn't hurt, could it?

Corey repressed a smile when she heard Matt's
artificial moan. She might have been out of the business for a while, but she hadn't lost her ability to
recognize a fake groan when she heard one. They
began their drive back to the Cape in almost total
silence. Unfortunately, now that the danger was clearly
over, her mind was free to wander. Thinking about
her past with Chuck or her present with Matt did
nothing to calm her nerves. Wanting to blot out the

sounds and memories that haunted her, Corey turned the radio on to a loud rock station. After a couple of minutes, she turned it down. "What kind of music do you like?" she asked. "I can change the channel."

"It's perfect. I was raised on the Beatles and the Rolling Stones, and I still like that. I figure as long as Mick Jagger and Tina Turner can keep rocking, so can I."

"That surprises me. I thought professors would only like classical music."

"I enjoy that, too. In fact, the only thing I don't like is opera. What about you?"

"My two real passions are rock and Broadway musicals."

"Really? I have a friend who lives in New York who has a copy of every *Playbill* ever published. He gets me tickets whenever I'm in town. Maybe we could go someday?" Matt asked, wanting and needing some reassurance that they had a future together. "Let's plan to go on the day I turn in my galleys to the publisher. In fact, let's overdose and see three or four in a week."

"Maybe," Corey muttered, smiling despite herself. She had to give Matt credit. He was certainly persistant. Moving to a safer topic, she asked if he thought that the musicals of the eighties were better or worse than the older traditional ones like *South Pacific*? Did he prefer *Cats* or *Phantom of the Opera* to *West Side Story*?

From that point on, they managed to keep their conversation light and casual all the way back to the Cape. Both were pleasurably surprised to find their tastes were similar, and they chatted as though they were old friends. Corey almost forgot to check for tails. Matt almost forgot that he had a great deal of explaining left to do.

It was after six when Corey pulled into the parking lot behind a fast-food restaurant near her shop. "I'm going to bring along a book next time," Matt complained good-naturedly. "All I ever do is sit and wait."

"You don't know the meaning of waiting in a car," Corey told him. "I've literally spent years waiting in trucks, vans, cars, and believe me, it doesn't begin to get uncomfortable until after the fourth or fifth hour."

"Sounds like your job wasn't all glamour and excitement."

"I'd hardly call any of it glamourous."

"What would you call it then?" Matt asked.

"How many tacos do you want, three or four?" Corey asked him, almost at the same time.

When Matt sat, staring at her, demanding an answer with his eyes, she grimaced and said, "If you really want to know, it was mostly boring and uncomfortable. When I wasn't bored, I was nervous or plain scared. Does that satisfy your blasted curiosity?" Before he could answer, she was out of the car. "Too late to choose," she told over her shoulder. "You'll have to eat whatever I buy."

Minutes later they were sitting next to each other at the kitchen table, eating the tacos and tostadas and burritos with their fingers. Corey grabbed a roll of paper towels, but they still managed to dribble hot sauce and cheese all over the table.

"Well . . ." Corey spoke into the awkward silence. "Dinner's over. I'll bring up your disks in the morning and you can get back to work." She stood up, gathering the bits of paper and stuffed them in the trash. "Go to bed. You've had a long day."

"Corey . . ." Matt began, moving toward her. "We need to talk about what happened."

"There's nothing to say. Don't ruin it." In a quietly desperate voice, she added, "We can be friends, if you'll let it go."

Seeing the anguish in her eyes, Matt reached over to touch her arm. "We already are friends, Corey. Nothing can change that. The rest will come." Knowing that this was not the time to push his luck further, he stroked her arm softly. "I'll see you in the morning."

With an almost audible sigh of relief, Corey nodded her head. "Remember not to come downstairs without hitting that button beside the third step." She would have felt much more at ease if Matt hadn't paused on his way to the stairs, giving her one of his warmest smiles, and added, "It's good to be home."

Hours later Corey lay in her narrow bed, tired but unable to sleep. What did Matt mean, the rest will come? That it was good to be home? There was no way that she would become involved with a man as a substitute for someone else. She was not, nor ever could be, his beloved Sally. She simply could not compete with a memory. When Corey realized that she was jealous, actually jealous of a dead woman, she whispered an ancient Hebrew curse to fate and to her own stupidity. She was much too close to loving this man. *Back away*, she ordered herself, *or I'll only get hurt again. Much worse than before*.

The next morning Matt waited until Corey was downstairs to emerge from his room. He stood in front of the bathroom mirror, inhaling the lingering fragrance of her bath oil while he performed his morning rituals. What was it about this woman that so fascinated him, Matt pondered as he pulled on a new pair of jeans. She was tall and slim, almost tomboyish in appearance, until you looked at the delicate bones and saw the beauty in those luminous azure eyes. Other women might be more obviously beautiful, more flamboyant, but none appealed to him as much.

"Come and get it," Corey yelled up from the kitchen as the smell of bacon and eggs drifted to his room. Pulling on his beige fisherman's knit sweater, Matt walked down, glad to find that his leg was close enough to normal that he wasn't automatically favoring it. Corey gave him a quick smile before he sat down, and Matt's mood improved dramatically.

"How's your leg?" she asked, her eyes inspecting him. He was slim and virile-looking, his black hair tousled and his blue eyes bright. With his cast off, nothing disturbed his dark appeal, his tight jeans and sweater accentuating his strength rather than concealing it. A few dark curls escaped from the top of his sweater, making him much too appealing.

"It seems better. It's great to have the cast off. I could roll over in bed last night without making a production out of it." Sighing, he said, "I wish I'd been able to sleep better. Corey, we have to talk."

Turning to face him with serious eyes, Corey agreed. "I know, Matt. We both deserve better than this terrible awkwardness. It was all right in the car, so we'll have to find a way to make it right with us here in the store. More ground rules, I suppose." Looking up, she made one request. "Can you wait until this evening? There'll be more time."

"Deal, Corey," Matt said, standing up and brushing her lips with his own. "For now I'll abide by the same rules as before. Stay out of sight until the shop is closed."

"Fine. But that means no more kissing," Corey admonished him as she stepped back from him. "We're going to have to be extra careful now," she told him, purposefully changing the subject. "Parker said that he rounded up the group in Boston, but I assume that their employers now know for sure that Boston is the hot spot, so to speak. They'll send out people all through New England, and sooner or later, they might find us, even by accident."

"I'll stay out of sight. Thanks for getting my disks," he said, taking the box that was sitting on the kitchen table. When she nodded, Matt walked out, pausing only to give her a brief smile, his mind already on the chapters that he planned to revise that morning.

The day passed uneventfully, with Corey inspecting each customer with wary eyes but finding nothing amiss. Ten minutes before the store closed that afternoon, the phone rang and Corey was pleased to hear the distinctive Irish brogue of her beloved godfather, Sean McCaulley. "Where have you been, Corey? I've been trying to reach you."

"Sorry, I had to make a quick trip into Boston. I should have called you, Sean, but things got a trifle hectic around here. Are you all right?" Corey asked, concern coloring her voice.

"I'm fine. How about you? You sound funny. Are you all right?"

"Everything's fine."

"Do you remember Lydia Sanders?" Sean asked, coming to the point of his call. "She's moving in here sometime next month. Her husband died two months ago, and she's finally decided to sell her house. It's that huge gabled two-story one that you've always loved down off Conner Point. Do you know which one?''

"Do you mean the gray Victorian? 'Our house?' "

"That's the one. Anyway, I persuaded her to let you have first refusal on the contents. I know you'll give a fair price, and it'll be easier than an auction for her if you can manage." Lowering his voice, he whispered, "I know it's full of really good stuff, Corey. I was in it once, years ago."

"Oh, Sean," Corey exclaimed, the antique dealer in her overshadowing all else for a few minutes. "That is an incredible opportunity. Does anyone else know about this? Is the house for sale, too?"

"It might be. Lydia is going to sell her furniture first and see if her nephew is interested in the house. If he's not, it'll probably go on the market. Will you go and make a bid?"

"Of course I will. This is a fantastic opportunity. When does she want it done?"

"As soon as possible. One of the reasons that she agreed to let you make an offer is that you're local and can be quick about it. She's on a short trip for this week and would like an offer when she gets back."

"I don't know if I can."

"Lydia isn't going to wait. She's an impulsive woman and wants an answer now. Look, Corey, you can't let this opportunity pass you by. Surely you can get a couple of hours to look. Are you sure you're all right?''

"Tell Mrs. Sanders that I'd be honored to make a

bid on her furniture. In fact, I might as well do an inventory of the major pieces while I'm at it.'' Making Sean suspicious surely would be more dangerous than doing a quick once over of the house. "How do I get in?"

"The key's under the flowerpot left of the garage."

"Thanks, Sean. I owe you two dinners for this."

"It's my pleasure, Corey. I'm always glad to help my favorite girl."

"And I'm always glad to hear from my favorite man," Corey told him, using the old ritual phrases that persisted from her childhood days.

Corey didn't notice Matt standing in the stairwell behind the shop, waiting for her to give him the all clear. She started when he moved behind her and cleared his throat to make his presence known. Corey wasn't surprised, however, to hear the sardonic note in his voice when he asked her, "Who was that? Who is your favorite man?"

Although she was briefly tempted to tease, to play feminine games with him, Corey answered truthfully. "Sean McCaulley, my godfather. I told you all about him."

"You did. I'm sorry I snapped. You sounded so happy, and . . ." Matt admitted sheepishly, "I was jealous." Seeing her defenses rise, Matt forestalled her next comment with a raised hand. "So, what was the good news?"

Forgetting to reprimand him, Corey turned and walked to the window, speaking in a soft voice that caused Matt to walk behind her in order to hear. "My favorite house in the whole world is going up on the market, and Sean got me permission to bid on the contents for the shop. I shouldn't leave you, but if I refuse, Sean will worry and send someone to check up on me. Going is safer than not. Besides . . . it might be a real opportunity.''

"Haven't you ever been in the house?"

"No, I've admired it every time I drove by. I'll probably hate the inside—at least I hope I do.''

"Why?"

"Because there is no way that I could afford to buy the house, and if it's as perfect inside as it is out, it'll drive me crazy to see some one else buy it and turn it into a bed-and-breakfast or tear it down.''

"It must be a good-size house.''

"Big enough for a huge family," Corey said wistfully.

"Is that what you want the house for?" Matt asked, speaking softly, calmly, knowing that Corey was revealing her dreams to him in a way that she normally wouldn't.

"That house deserves a lot of kids and dogs. You know, I always thought of it as my house, when I was a little girl and we visited here on the Cape. Sean would drive me over there and I would dream about it. I was going to live there someday with five kids, and two dogs and one cat.''

"Was there a husband in your dream?"

"Of course," Corey said, surprised at what she'd said. She hadn't thought of the old house in years, and no one but Sean ever knew of her childhood dreams. "Every little girl assumes that a tall, dark, handsome prince, complete with white horse, will sweep her off her feet and they'll live happily ever after. But that isn't the real world, is it?"

"No, Corey," Matt said solemnly. "The real world throws us twists and curves that we don't always want or need. But that doesn't mean you give up your dreams. You modify them, that's all. And when they come true, they mean a great deal more to you than if they'd come easily.''

When Corey shrugged and turned to walk toward the stove, Matt asked her if he could go with her to see her dream house. ''I'll help you do the inventory, Corey. I'm good at taking notes and we could make quick work of it together. Besides, I'd really like to help you for a change, after all you've done for me.''

After a moment, she shook her head. ''Okay,'' she told him. ''You've got yourself a deal. I'll fix dinner and we can go over after dark. I don't think anyone will see you.'' Corey found herself agreeing for a variety of reasons, not the least of which was that they might avoid talking if they found themselves too busy taking inventory.

''There it is,'' Corey announced as she pulled into the driveway. The three-story clapboard house was perched on a promontory overlooking the ocean, and mist surrounded them in eerie shadows as Corey turned off the headlights. The house loomed over them to the left, and the sound of waves on rocks assaulted their ears from all sides.

''It's a good thing I'm not afraid of ghosts. Are you sure, absolutely sure, that Norman Bates isn't lurking around here?''

Giving him a nasty look over her shoulder, Corey climbed out of the car. She clicked on her flashlight and walked briskly to the garage, finding the key where Sean had promised.

''I was kidding, just kidding,'' Matt said as he saw her frown. ''Can't you take a joke?''

''This isn't funny. The only reason I'm here is to keep Sean and his big mouth shut. And we should be relatively safe. Once the PF finds out what happened in Boston, they'll regroup and start again. I figure we have a day or two of grace in the meantime. After that, we're back to full security. All right with you?'' Corey asked, standing still until Matt nodded his acceptance. Only then did Corey resume walking up to the door.

"How old is this house anyway?" Matt asked, deliberately changing the subject as he approached the massive structure.

"It was built, I think, in the early 1800s by a prosperous sea captain. I'll ask Mrs. Sanders when I talk to her, or Sean. He knows more about this part of the Cape than anybody I know. Come on, it's damp out here," Corey directed as she walked up to the wide porch and unlocked the door. "Does the weather make your leg ache?"

Matt shook his head negatively and walked up the porch behind Corey. The house had a generous veranda surrounding it, decorated with what seemed to be carved wood trim. "Hey . . ." Matt requested, "will you shine the light over here for a moment? This porch is unbelievable."

"Later."

After they entered the house, Corey quickly snapped on the light in the entry hall. They both caught their breath at their first glimpse into the old house.

Polished wood gleamed everywhere, illuminated by the chandelier that hung down from the second floor. A curved staircase led to the upper floor and several doors opened onto the main floor of the house. A lovely table sat in the hall, with a matching chair, looking oddly incongruous with a modern Touch Tone telephone sitting on it. A grandfather clock loomed to the left of the door and Corey gasped out loud as she glanced at it, moving to examine it more closely when Matt spoke.

"It's a regular mansion. I had no idea that sea captains lived so well."

"I imagine the house has been added on to over the years," Corey noted absently to Matt as she inspected the clock. "These old homes are in constant states of repair and additions. This one looks like it's in excellent shape. Much better than I would have thought. They eat up money, though, even if you do lots of the work yourself."

Letting her eyes drift over the rest of the hall in appreciation, Corey summoned her professional self, and briskly said, "Let's get started. We'll article each room counterclockwise. First write down the room. When I give you a number and description, write it down. I've got my prenumbered tags to stick on each of the items as we proceed. I want to get a rough inventory tonight so I can check out any prices I'm not sure of later. I can look up recent listings for prices when we get back home. Have you got a pad or do you want mine?"

Three hours later, Corey sat down and told Matt, "If Mrs. Sanders needs money, her troubles are over." Standing up, she said, "I've done all I can tonight, but I can't resist seeing the rest of the house. Let's go upstairs and see what else is here. Just for fun."

"By all means. Lead on. I've always had my best fun in the bedroom."

"Cut it out, Stone," Corey told him, her danger signals flashing at the tone in his voice. "We're friends, that's all."

"For now," Matt told her, following her up the curved staircase to a large landing and hall that split on either side of the open area. "But not forever."

All six bedrooms were decorated in a similar fashion, and Corey had a mental list of "finds" that got longer and longer as she went from one room to the other. As she enthused over yet another dry sink in the third bedroom, Matt asked her what she liked best. "Would you like to live here with this furniture or do you see it as belonging in a museum?" he added.

After thinking for a moment, Corey answered honestly. "Some of both, I think. I find the furniture beautiful, but I wouldn't want to live in this house the way it is. It's too nice. I couldn't imagine a child having such beautiful things in her room, for example. Kids should be able to live with their things, not worry over a few scratches here or there. For that matter, I'd be almost afraid to live with some of this stuff myself." Pausing, Corey asked Matt much the same question. "How do you like the house? It must be very different from what you're used to. I imagine you living in a modern place back in California. All chrome and glass and water beds."

"I like this house very much, though I agree that the furniture is a bit too much to live with on an every-day basis. Despite all the fancy furniture, it seems like a home, rather than a house. You're right, by the way, about where I live in California. It's just a house that I live in, not a home where I belong."

Softly, he went on. "I once had a home, though, even if it looked a lot different than this one. What it had was the same feeling. Maybe . . ." Matt said softly, "it is the people more than the place that makes a house turn into a home." Taking a deep breath, Matt added, "When my wife and son died four years ago, my home turned back into a house

and I sold it. I couldn't live with the memories. Now
I live in a town house.''

A dead silence lasted while Corey struggled with
her emotions. She wasn't expecting him to mention
his wife, not here, where her defenses were down
and she forgot to keep him at arm's length. And a
son, he'd lost a son as well. Parker hadn't told her
that, doubtless thinking it wasn't information relevent
to his security clearance. For a solid minute, Corey
remained still. She didn't know what to say or what
to think.

Straightening her spine, Corey slowly turned to
face Matt, looking directly into his anxious blue
eyes. Control settled over her face. ''You've made
your point,'' she told him. ''We need to talk, and I
think you've made it clear that now is the time. Shall
we go back first?''

When Matt nodded, his eyes intent on her face,
Corey turned and walked through the house, turning
off the lights and securing it. He couldn't tell what
she was thinking; her face had settled into a mask
soon after he mentioned Sally. They drove in silence
back to the shop, and Corey didn't break it until she
unlocked her door and offered ''Coffee?'' in a strange
tone of voice.

Corey was going through the motions, stunned by
his announcement and its effect on her. For the past
couple of hours she'd been totally absorbed in the
exploration of the wonderful old house. Now reality
descended, all at once. Her past, his past. Death on
both sides. He'd lost not only a wife, but a son, and
Corey had let several wives and children die, through
her inaction. He felt compelled to tell her, after that
mistake in the motel, even if she didn't want to hear,
even when she didn't want to care about him. There

was no way that she could remain impassive if he opened his soul to her.

Matt sat in front of the fireplace, gazing into the kindling. Restlessly, he moved to start the fire and then, unable to sit, paced back and forth. He could hear Corey moving dishes in the kitchen, but he didn't quite know what to do. He had to let her come to him. They had to talk. *Why, you idiot,* he berated himself, *did you tell her that now*? He hadn't planned to tell her about Sally that night—not in such an abrupt way—but his mouth had opened and it was too late to retrieve the words. Too late to plan an elaborate speech.

EIGHT

When Matt thought that he could wait no more, the door opened. Corey walked carefully into the room, carrying a tray with a pot of coffee, two cups and saucers, and a small plate of cookies. Without further comment, she sat down and prepared to pour. Her movements were controlled, and Matt could only guess at the effort it took for her to remain expressionless.

Before she could utter a word, he spoke. "I'm sorry. I never meant to force you to listen to me, not like this. It just came out, I don't know why."

"I'm sorry, too. I didn't know about your son," Corey told him softly, not able to imagine the pain involved in losing a child. "What happened?" Corey asked, clutching at the facts, as though they could banish away the myriad of emotions that were flowing through her mind. And the unwanted pictures: Matt and a beautiful woman standing together holding a baby. A child, a beautiful boy with Matt's black hair, laughing, loving.

Matt watched Corey's face move, saw fear and sorrow and joy flicker across her eyes and he began to hope for the future. At least she cared. *Slowly*, he told himself, *go slowly. Start with her questions and work from there. Maybe she will forgive you for calling her Sally.* The old nightmares came back that night in Boston, triggered by the danger and excitement, he supposed. Then, like a fool, he had mistaken his new love for his old. It was no excuse, only an apology.

Poking the fire to give himself some time, Matt ordered himself to be careful. If he blew this chance, there would not be another. "Four years ago Sally and Tommy were blown up in an airplane, by terrorists. The PF took credit for it," he said slowly, the pain still rippling through his voice. "I doubt you remember the exact incident, there have been so many. We were all in Greece for the summer. They were going to fly back early. Tommy was starting kindergarten and Sally had to register for classes. I was going to follow them in a week, as soon as the university where I was teaching was done with its term."

"Matt . . ." Corey whispered, her eyes filled with tears. "I'm so sorry." Now Corey understood everything—his book, his nearly suicidal flirtation with danger, and most of all his determination to expose the PF. It was all an effort to attone for his family.

"So am I," he rasped, tears filling his voice. "I should have been with them, but I wasn't." The guilt that he'd carried for so long bubbled to the surface. "I should have kept them back with me."

"You couldn't have known. It wasn't your fault." The words were torn from her throat, forcing themselves past the pain that made the words feel like shards of glass. Others had said the same words to her. They hadn't helped her, but Corey hoped now she might find a way to make them mean something. This situation was all too similar to her own. Except she could have prevented her incident. Matt had nothing to do with the one that destroyed his family. "It could have been your plane instead. Any plane."

"I was the one who wanted to teach in Greece that summer," Matt went on. "If it wasn't for me, they'd be alive in California now. Tommy would be nine years old."

"Matt, Matt," Corey said, walking to him and cradling his head in her chest. She stood next to the chair where he sat, and held him, stroking the top of his head with a gentle hand and resting her cheek on his soft black hair. "You couldn't have known. No one could have known."

Taking a deep breath, Matt put his hands on Corey's gentle ones. "Damn it, Corey. I'm sorry for this," Matt said, trying to pull away. "I don't seem to do anything right when it comes to you. I thought I was all through with this."

"It never goes away, it just hides," Corey whispered. "It gets better, and it gets farther away, but the pain never leaves you. You don't want to forget your Sally and your. . . ." Corey swallowed, trying to remain strong, "son." Corey cursed herself, feeling ashamed of the red hot shaft of pain and jealousy that ran through her at the thought of some other woman having his son. That was what she wanted, what she yearned for with a deep passion. She closed her eyes in pain when she comprehended her thoughts, what she'd been forced to admit to herself in this emotional firestorm.

Corey whispered into his hair, holding him with arms of steel. "Your book, on terrorists . . . that's your penance for Sally?"

"No, not penance," Matt asserted, pulling away to look at Corey's tear-glazed eyes. "It's my way of stopping them, my small effort at exposing the animals who so ruthlessly destroy innocent lives.

"The year after they were killed, I started a file on the PF. I wanted to do something, anything. Nothing much came of my research until last year. One of my students, the son of a wealthy Saudi, took my class— and really listened to me. He came to see me privately, and put me in touch with my informant. After all the years, I could finally do something to make a difference." With glowing blue eyes, Matt fiercely petitioned her. "You, of all people, don't believe in forgiving the criminals who live that way?"

"No, of course I don't. I've spent all my adult life trying to stop people like that, for all the good it's done. I can understand your need for vengeance. More than vengeance," she corrected herself, "more to stop them from ever doing it again. I understand it more than you could ever know," she whispered, thinking of all the unvented anger she'd felt when she'd heard that the terrorists she'd been monitoring had hijacked that bus. "I can see why this book is so important to you." Pausing, she reached down to place a hand on Matt's rough cheek. "It will help, too. You know who's really behind it, and exposing them has to help. Sooner or later the world will stop tolerating this behavior, and you will have helped."

"My sweet Corey, what did I do to deserve you? I meant to talk, to apologize for calling you Sally, to ease your pain, and . . . you ease mine instead." Pulling her down to his lap, Matt circled her waist with one arm and used his hand to bring her lips to his, murmuring her name over and over before his lips touched hers.

Hot, sweet passion exploded between them, their lips touching off an inferno beneath the skin. Thought fled from Corey's mind as the touch of his lips on hers fueled needs and wants that were so new as to be overwhelming. Some part of her stayed sane for the first moment, and her small internal voice warned her that she would pay. But Corey didn't care. Whatever the price, whatever the payment, it didn't matter at that moment. Her burning need and aching heart didn't care. Their thundering cut out all thoughts that didn't include Matt and the sensations that were burning within her.

Hunger and lightning flashed as Corey turned to wildfire in Matt's arms, their bodies searing the clothes between them. Matt gathered her into his arms and eased them down to the thick carpet before the roaring fire. For a dazed moment he wondered if the fire was pouring out over them until he realized that the heat was all their own, made brighter by the wait, made hotter by the emotions that were loose within them.

Matt's mouth took possession of Corey's as he lay beside her, his tongue finding a mate in hers. Their lips melted together, each needing to learn the other's mysteries. As Matt boldly reached under her shirt to cup her swelling breasts, Corey moved her hand under his sweater, seeking his burning flesh. Clothing fell away as they suddenly began to pull and tug on zippers and buttons. As Matt's mouth sought Corey's, she pressed her pliant body to his hard strength, her breasts tingling with the delight of his flesh, with the teasing eroticism of his soft hair rubbing on her tender nipples.

Unable to resist, wanting to touch and taste all of Corey at once, Matt ran a string of fast, hard kisses down her neck. Corey's body convulsed with pleasure as his mouth settled over her ruby-hard nipple, overwhelmed by the thrilling sensations that his tongue and teeth induced. Clasping his head to her, Corey urged him on, lost to the feelings that she was learning, enjoying, cherishing.

Corey's unrestrained response put an end to the last remnant of Matt's control. He had promised himself to make it perfect, beautiful, their first time together, but need got in the way, need that demanded satisfaction.

Corey was a stranger in her body. Pulses of fire were surging through her body, demanding, insistent sensations that could not be ignored. A yearning burned in her body that was rapidly becoming so overwhelming that she felt as though she would gladly die to satisfy. When Matt's hand first touched her thigh, she moved toward him, her muscles rippling uncontrollably, wanting and needing his touch more than the very air she breathed.

Groaning, Matt managed to raise his lips for a moment, gazing into Corey's passion-torn face. "Now, my Corey, now," he told her. With the bit of control that remained, he purposefully mentioned her name just as he entered her body. He wanted her to always remember that he knew who she was—that the first time they made love, she had not been a substitute for anyone.

"Make me yours," Corey moaned into his mouth. She reached up to cup his head, pulling him down onto her, taking the sweet weight of his body over hers, where he could sense her hot, wet readiness. With a slow movement, Matt entered her body, surprised at the tightness. He stopped when he heard Corey's small moan. "Am I hurting you, Corey?"

he whispered. Shaking her head, unable to talk, Corey reached and put her arms around the small of Matt's back. Her answer was to pull him down, down farther into her, while she arched her body to fully receive him. "God, Corey," Matt moaned before he, too, lost all ability to talk.

Time lost its meaning as their bodies blended together, moving with grace as their separate needs fanned each other's. Corey instinctively moved to find the rhythm to match Matt's and they found a perfect synchronization that started slowly and built up to a crescendo that sent shudders of sparks bursting inside Corey's entire body. As Matt felt the first contractions that signaled Corey's satisfaction, his body reacted and joined hers, in a place new to them both. Corey felt the entire universe move within her, the boundaries of her world coalesce into a small point that exploded back to reality with millions of points of fire, shimmering and echoing through her body.

As reality returned, first to Matt and then to Corey, they clasped each other tightly, not wanting anything to mar the perfection. When Corey shivered, Matt realized that he would have to do something. Tenderly he removed his body from hers, kissing first her forehead, nose, then lips as he moved away.

"Corey . . ." he began when her eyes touched his. Wide with wonder and pleasure, the dusky blue was turned dark with desire and satisfaction. And with entreaty. Understanding the look without words, Matt knew that she wanted nothing to spoil this moment.

Matt slowly stood, and gazed down at the woman at his feet. She was exquisite, Matt thought, as his eyes caressed her. Corey lay, relaxed in a way she had thought was impossible. Her every bone was liquid, surrounded by soft skin and transparent muscle. She was a leaf floating in a sea of honey, no longer able to move. When Corey saw the tenderness in Matt's eye, she gloried in his look and languidly reached up to cup one of her breasts, enjoying the heat grow in his eyes as she did.

Lying there, she looked up to examine her lover. He was magnificent, tall, dark, and intensely masculine. His skin was bronzed, except for one narrow white bathing suit mark across his loins. Slowly, she reached over to caress his ankle, wanting to touch as well as see. As she moved her hand up the leg, tenderly stroking the back of his knee, an iron hand grasped her softer one.

"Come, Corey. Now," Matt ordered as he pulled her to her feet. With weak legs, she stood, leaning her head against his chest. As his arms settled around her, she snuggled into him, dipping her head so that she could find the small, masculine nipple within the forest on his chest. As her tongue snaked out to touch the tip of it, marveling as it changed under her touch, Matt groaned.

"You witch," he rasped as he walked toward the stairs, pulling her behind him. After they reached his bedroom, he turned to her, pressing his fully aroused body to hers once more. "I want you again, Corey," he whispered against her ear, nibbling small bites, touching the tender skin with the tip of his tongue. "Come to me, now."

Tender desire shining from her eyes, Corey turned to Matt and opened her arms. "Lucky . . ." she managed to whisper. "I seem to want you again, too. More and more. . . ." she confessed as his lips touched the peak of her breast and his arms cradled

her. As she leaned, knees weak with desire, Matt
supported her as they walked the rest of the way to
the double bed, pausing briefly to strip back the
covers with one hand. When she turned to him, Matt
settled her gently on the cool pink sheets, spreading
her legs as he knelt between them. For a long moment, he gazed at her—wanton woman, loved woman,
wanting woman. Groaning, he reached down, claiming her mouth with his own.

Needs grew to impossible levels, fueled by his
fingers as they, too, explored and worshiped. When
he entered her, Corey felt her body grasp his, ripples
of pleasure radiating like starbursts as she shimmered
in ecstasy. It was too soon, Matt thought, too soon,
but he could not restrain himself. When Corey's
body began to quiver around his hardness, he joined
her in their elemental celebration of life and love. At
peace, they fell asleep, cradled in each other's arms.

As the pale light of dawn crept into the room, Matt
stirred, instinctively pulling Corey closer to him. His
eyes tenderly followed the line of her slender form
under the sheet, noting with satisfaction his hand
curving possessively around her hip. Brushing the
tousled curls from her forehead with his lips, he
waited for her to awaken, wanting her anew.

Corey awoke feeling strangely safe, wanting to
stay in the lovely warmth of her dream. She felt a
warm breath in her ear and opened her eyes to find
Matt's gaze intently devouring her own. When she
opened her mouth to express her surprise, or joy, or
fear, Matt captured it. Corey never knew what she
would have said, never remembered the words that
were buried under his passion. She was lost in the
tide of need that Matt's touch rekindled.

She burned when Matt's mouth captured her breast

and let the fingers of her hand run like water through his silken hair. She gloried in the feel of his strong, muscular body against hers. As her blood began to sizzle, burning new pathways in her body, Corey felt a small trace of wonder and then fear. Never in her life had she felt so greedy, so incomplete. How was it possible to want so much, to need so desperately?

Sensing her trace of panic, Matt soothed her with a gentle kiss, whispering his need. When she sighed in response, Matt captured her mouth with his and joined their bodies with a swift motion. Suddenly her body tightened around his, bringing them both to an ecstasy that was made all the sweeter by the fact that they were together. Still joined in every way, arms and legs tangled wantonly, they fell into a deep, satisfied sleep.

Corey awoke two hours later when she heard the faint buzzing of an alarm in a distant room. Trapped by a heavy weight, she instinctively pushed herself free. She landed on her feet beside the bed before she realized what she had done. As Matt watched, Corey's world tilted. She remembered last night and that morning and stood, rooted in indecision. Finally Matt reached out his hand toward her. "You're beautiful. This is beautiful."

Corey ran. Out of her bedroom, back to the room she'd occupied since Matt's arrival. She turned off the buzzing alarm and threw on the first sweatshirt and jeans she grabbed. When she finished pulling up her warm socks, she sat down on the bed Indian-fashion.

Contradictions fought within her. She gloried in her response to Matt and the splendor he'd opened to her. Yet nothing good could come of it. She didn't deserve Matt, didn't deserve the pleasure he offered. Thankfully, there was no reason to think that last night meant anything special to Matt. It was only her own conceit that measured last night as something important. With Matt's looks, he'd probably had scores of women. No one made love as expertly as that man did without lots of practice. And it was clear from that night in Boston that his dead wife was still the woman he truly loved. She was just one of many women passing through the professor's bed. As usual, she had overreacted and made too much out of a minor matter. This behavior could not be repeated, as enjoyable and as educational as it was. It was unprofessional.

By the time Corey turned to go downstairs and open the shop, she'd convinced herself they could be able to return to their previously friendly relationship and ignore last night entirely. It was nearly ten o'clock, and, by the rules, she wouldn't have to see Matt until lunch. That would give her all the time she needed to rehearse a speech that would let Matt down easy and keep him far, far away from her in the future.

Matt lay on his back, sighing as he watched Corey retreat through the doorway. He hoped that she might come to him but wasn't surprised when she hadn't. Never had a woman so stirred his blood or shared such a profound passion with him. He felt as though his very being had been shaken, changed by the experience. If he were so upset, then she had to be. Only in her case, those feelings were obviously frightening her instead of bringing her the deep satisfaction that they were bringing him. With a sardonic bit of insight, Matt realized that although Corey was an expert in some matters, she was terribly naive when it came to love and sex. It was going to take every bit of his patience and understanding to crack through the rest of Corey's protective barriers.

But he would. He had to. For the second time in his life he was deeply, irrevocably in love. Why, he wondered as he took a slow shower, had he fallen in love with this particular woman, so different from his first wife? Perhaps, he finally concluded as the hot water ran out, his second chance at love was inevitably bound to be more complex than the simple joys of young love. With a twinge of guilt he accepted the fact that his second love was destined to be deeper and more meaningful as well.

Walking freely for the first time in ten weeks, he did a quick series of stretching exercises to determine the extent of his physical deterioration. Smiling, he let himself dwell for a moment on the impish good humor that lurked under Corey's serious demeanor.

On the night before he ruined his cast they'd sat watching television, trying to find something that interested them both. Matt's fingers had stopped at the same time Corey spoke, both of them caught by a tennis match.

"Do you play?" she'd idly inquired.

"Not well, but with enthusiasm. How about you?"

"I haven't for several years, but I was pretty serious about it in college. I almost joined the circuit."

"Why didn't you?"

"Parker thought I'd be too visible."

"I should have guessed. Have you ever regretted it?"

"No. I probably was never good enough."

Matt muttered a most descriptive Arabic curse at that point, explaining when Corey raised an eyebrow at his reaction. "Parker had too much to do with your life—none of it good."

"Well, he did send you here, didn't he?" Corey had drawled with a quirky smile.

"All right, but one out of a thousand isn't enough to lend him my approval. I don't like men like that; they take themselves altogether too seriously."

"Why? Why didn't you take all of this more seriously? From what I heard, for a very bright man, you took a lot of chances."

"I didn't want to believe I was in danger, I guess. And, before I met you, maybe I wasn't too concerned for my safety. I haven't been looking forward to the future much, until now."

"Matt. All this is all temporary, until your book is done and the cast can come off." With a bubble of silly laughter, she told him, "Think of it as a 'castivity,' a captivity caused by plaster."

They had laughed together then, and the momentary seriousness had been avoided. Tennis captured their attention and the rest of the evening had been spent eating popcorn and analyzing tennis strokes. When Matt extracted a promise from Corey that they would play together someday, he had smiled in gentle satisfaction. When Corey was not thinking directly about the future, she unthinkingly made plans with him. This told Matt two important things: that she enjoyed his company and that she wanted a future with him, whether she could admit it to herself or not.

The smell of hot coffee finally broke into Matt's consciousness. He quickly finished buttoning his light-blue shirt. After pulling a navy sweater over it, he started down the stairs. Barefoot, he silently walked into the kitchen, his eyes resting in satisfaction on Corey's blond head and slim body. He walked over to her and slowly put an arm around her, leaning down to nuzzle into her neck. "Morning, love,"

Matt greeted her, frowning when she stiffened and pulled herself away.

Not surprisingly, Corey the agent snapped, "What are you doing down here now?"

"I smelled the coffee and couldn't resist," Matt announced, deciding not to add anything personal. "I'll stay out of the shop. Now that my leg's better, can't I come down to the back during the day?"

"I'd prefer that you work. The sooner your book's done, the better. For us both."

"What does that crack mean?" Matt asked, losing a grip on his temper. He'd planned on giving her some space, but not this much. "What the hell is going on? You're acting like nothing happened between us last night. As if we didn't make passionate love this morning. Like you never wrapped your legs around me and wanted me in you."

"Don't be crude," Corey snapped.

"It wasn't crude, it was wonderful. That's what makes this whole conversation a farce. Don't tell me it meant nothing to you. I was there, lady, and you won't convince me that it was no big deal to you."

"Well, it wasn't any big deal," Corey drawled in her most sardonic voice. "You were good—but not great."

With a swiftness that surprised Corey, Matt strode over to her and deliberately grabbed her arms with his large hands. Holding her a prisoner, he looked directly into her startled blue eyes. "Throw me over your shoulder if you want, but don't you dare lie to me, Corey Hamilton. Don't you dare lie to yourself. I won't let you! Last night was special, unbelievably wonderful. No one has ever made me feel the way you do, and I know that no man has ever touched you the way I did."

Looking up into blazing blue eyes, Corey let her gaze drift down past his strong nose to the sensual lips that were parted in anger. Corey deliberately stared at the bookcase behind Matt, trying to read the titles, telling herself to think of cold showers, rolling around in icebanks—anything to take her mind off him and last night. If just looking at him and hearing his raspy voice could melt through her defenses, how would she ever convince him to leave her alone? Panic gave her the courage to try again, to somehow convince Matt to leave her alone.

"How could you tell that, Stone? You forget my past. I might have slept with a hundred men, a thousand, and learned to fake it very well. They teach it in spy school, Sex 109. How to play an innocent." Seeing the doubt in his eyes, she pressed on, taunting, "Want to know what they call Sex 209? That's not for amateurs like you. Or sex 309, leather and chains?"

For a second, Matt faltered, wondering if anyone could be that good an actress. But he faltered for only a second. Corey wasn't experienced with men, he knew it. When he saw the tiniest flicker of pain in her eye, he pulled her to him, holding her tighter than she'd ever been held before.

"No, Corey, no one is that good an actress. Good try, though. I'm glad that your sense of humor hasn't left you as well as your common sense." Pausing, he put his hand under her chin and forced her to look into his eyes. When she finally met his gaze, he touched her cheek with one finger. "What we have is real and good, and I won't let it end." Letting her go, he added, "Go and tend to your shop. Think about it. Think about me. Think about how good we are together. We'll talk tonight."

As Corey obeyed, she wondered how Matt had suddenly gained control of her life. She was supposed to be the agent and he was supposed to be the subject. Things had gotten out of hand, and she was helpless against him. A wave of weakness hit her as she recalled his words about their lovemaking. Desire ran through her, hot and heavy, as she thought of last night. She had revealed too much then, but it was too late to change that. Now she had to think carefully and see what could be salvaged out of this situation. Was there any way she could come out of this predicament unscathed? Matt would have smiled if he heard her thoughts. Despite her protests, Corey finally admitted, at least to herself, that they did have a relationship.

NINE

The shop was unusually busy that day. The weather had turned mild and several daytrippers from Boston broused happily and bought freely. Normally Corey would have been pleased, but not today. Whenever she wasn't busy, she composed little speeches, telling Matt their night could never be repeated. Unfortunately, whenever she remembered his touch, her knees grew weak with longing. Somehow, though, she was determined to end it all.

Luscious odors began drifting into the shop after five o'clock. Obviously Matt had decided that a good dinner would further seduce her. It wouldn't. With deliberate movements she closed the shop, swearing she would be strong.

Matt stood in the kitchen, an apron tied over a pair of skintight jeans and a soft cashmere sweater that was exactly the color of his eyes. He looked ridiculously tempting, barefoot in her kitchen, his long dark hair slightly disheveled, as though he'd run his fingers through it. Without thinking, Corey's devilish sense of humor broke the awkward silence. "I don't suppose this means you're pregnant?"

Their laughter blended with the homey smells of

the simmering spaghetti sauce. The house was turning into a home for them both as Matt glanced at his bare feet, his dirty apron, and then, the woman that he'd pulled into his arms.

"Can't we compromise? I'll stay barefoot and in the kitchen, and I'll get you pregnant." With a sudden drawn breath, Matt realized what he'd said, and more importantly, that he'd meant every word. As Corey stiffened, he knew that she was not yet ready for anything even bordering on permanence. Not yet, anyway. Sooner or later, he vowed, she would be his. His woman. His wife. Pregnant with his child.

"Will you settle for a home-cooked dinner now and then?" he asked her, leaning down to place a light kiss on her parted lips.

"At least for tonight. You're a better cook than I am."

"Then please sit down, m'lady, and let me serve you," Matt lisped in a phony Italian accent. Pressing a glass of chilled Chablis in her hand, he settled her down in her chair, bowed from the waist, and informed her that dinner would be served in ten minutes. "Would madam care for an hors d'oeuvre before her dinner, or would she rather have," Matt asked with a hopeful leer, "a kiss from the chef?"

Giving Corey no chance to answer, he swooped down to capture her lips with his own. What started out as a light caress turned fiery, and Matt's lips rubbed sensually against hers, his tongue licking first one corner and then the other. Unable to resist, Corey's lips parted for his, eager for the blend of warm wine and the subtle taste that belonged alone to her lover. Matt leaned further down, settling on his knees before Corey, taking her into his arms.

With deliberate skill, Matt teased her, first thrusting his tongue into her mouth, then softly nibbling on her lower lip, alternating between seductive teasing and small bites of passion. Finally she could resist no more, and she wrapped her arms around Matt's powerful torso, pulling their bodies into contact. Sensuously rubbing her breasts against his chest, Corey thrust her tongue into his mouth.

Finally Matt pulled back, supremely satisfied with the results of his lovemaking. Corey lay in his arms, her eyes softened by desire, her body boneless against his. "I'm glad you settled for this kind of hors d'oeuvre. The only other choice was a jar of stale cashews." Then he stood up and announced that dinner would be ready in five minutes.

"What in the devil is all this about?" Corey blazed as she looked up at the satisfied smile on his face. "Is this a joke to you? Playing macho again?"

"It was no joke. I wanted to make a point, my dear ex-agent," Matt explained, suddenly dead serious. "I know you spend the entire day in your shop, trying to find ways to get away from me. I bet you made up at least fifty different ways of telling me that this relationship isn't going to work, and that we can't be lovers anymore. If I'm right, nod your head."

Matt waited a second while Corey reluctantly nodded.

Walking back to her, Matt grabbed her hand, pressing it to his aroused body for a brief moment. "Feel that and tell me that you think I'm joking," he demanded, his voice husky. "I want you more than I've ever wanted any other woman in my life. Is that blunt enough?" Corey nodded again, her mouth unable to form a coherent word. For a brief moment, she had felt the throbbing hardness barely constrained by the rough denim of his pants. Her fingers had instinctively cupped around the shape, and she longed to feel the satiny smooth skin that her hand shaped.

"Now, do you understand me? It's too late to fight it. We are lovers and we're going to stay lovers. You want me and I want you. You can complain all you want, we can talk about it all during dinner, but the basic premise is unchanged. First we are going to eat, Corey," Matt informed her. "Then we are going to go upstairs and make love. Wonderfully."

Deciding that the tall ebony-haired man who stood glaring at her had a most valid point, that actions did speak louder than words, Corey rose to her feet and put her arms around his neck. "If we are to be lovers, let's start now." With that, she used her tongue to explore the tender convolutions of his ear while her fingers slipped beneath the waistband of his jeans and sought the satin hardness that had so tantalized her moments ago.

"To hell with dinner," Matt murmured, sweeping her into his arms, "I want dessert now."

"Put me down, you crazy man," Corey demanded laughingly, nipping the lobe of Matt's ear lightly. "I can walk. I don't want you to fall and hurt your other leg."

"Okay, crazy lady," Matt whispered back. "I'll let you walk, but only if I can be behind you." When Corey agreed with a sigh, Matt slid her down his body, slowly rubbing her soft breasts against his hard, muscular torso. Then he turned her around, and, his arms confining her, they started up the stairs. Corey was lost in a haze of desire and was willing to acquiesce to Matt's every need. Her doubts were all silent, the desire that surged through her body drowning out all but the need that screamed to be satisfied.

Matt didn't allow any lull in his seduction, using

his long arms and limber fingers to reach around her waist. By the time Corey had reached the third step, Matt had unbuttoned and unzipped her jeans. With clever fingers, he eased them down to her hips, and urging her to stop briefly, he pulled them entirely free of her body on the next two steps, one leg a step.

Corey felt her bones melting as his warm fingers slightly grazed the back of her delicate lace panties. When she faltered, Matt stepped up behind her. Her head resting on his shoulder, he was one step behind her. With slow deliberation, Matt hooked the edge of her panties and left them, discarded with her jeans, on the next step. When Corey felt his warm fingers edge up the back of her sweatshirt, she sighed. The roughness of his jeans, the heated masculinity that was contained within, both rubbed seductively on her bare bottom. Corey was barely able to climb the last two steps, her knees too weak to support her. She felt as though the central portion of her body had turned into molten lava.

As they reached the top of the landing, Corey turned into Matt's embrace and he slipped off her sweatshirt. Corey stood, clasped in his arms, totally naked except for a sheer bra. With slightly fumbling fingers, Matt unhooked that last barrier and took her into his arms again, this time carrying her without protest into her bedroom.

Matt stripped off the bedspread and laid Corey in the middle of her pale-pink sheets. They could hear the ocean pounding in the background, sea gulls screaming as they searched for the last catch of the day. Corey knew that she would always remember that moment in time. An occasional car, and muted street sounds shattered the silence that grew more and more heated as Matt stood, his eyes traveling up and down her, taking in each and every inch of Corey's quivering body. Walking over, he straightened one of her legs, moving it slightly to the side so that her femininity was open and available for his worshipful appreciation.

Watching her eyes, he moved to stand at her feet, reaching for the first button of his shirt. Slowly, he stripped off his clothing, never letting his eyes leave hers. When he was down to his brief bikini underwear, underwear that was now grossly inadequate, he at last broke the silence, speaking in a deepened husky voice. "I want you, Corey, more than I've ever wanted another woman."

Corey lay there, feeling more erotic than she thought any woman could, watching her lover undress before her. When he finally stripped off his underwear, demanding her to tell him that she was an active participant in their lovemaking, insisting that she say it out loud, for both their sakes, she had been unable to restrain herself. Her voice came out in a low growl. "Come to me, Matt. Now."

With a smile that was almost pained, Matt heard her confess her desire and breathed a sigh of relief. This relentless seduction had been a calculated risk, but it was the only way he knew to break through Corey's defenses. Things hadn't gone exactly as planned, but the main objective—making her want him as much as he wanted her—had worked beyond his wildest dreams.

The trouble was that as Matt seduced her, so she had enticed him. Now he was so wild for her, he didn't know if he could wait long enough to satisfy her. Corey, sensing the hesitation in his eyes, reached up a slightly trembling hand to touch him. "Come to me, Matt. I want you. Inside me. Don't make me wait anymore."

With a groan he wasn't able to supress, Matt covered her slender body with his, thrusting his tongue into her mouth to drink the sweetness that he needed to exist. Their bodies slid together, fitting perfectly. Corey moved her legs, accommodating him before he knew. Neither expected the passion that had surfaced in Corey. Nothing could have pleased either of them more.

Time stopped and the sound of the ocean disappeared. All that was left for Corey was the satin warmth that bloomed within her, and the touch of Matt's body on hers. As they forged together, waves of feelings cascaded over Corey, sweeping her body into a whirlpool of sensation. Matt followed her into the swirling explosion.

Matt collasped onto Corey's sweat-slickened body, slowly rubbing their chests together. Reaching down, he smoothed her hair from her moist brow and gave her a tender kiss. Reluctantly, he pulled himself from her warmth and moved to her side, enfolding her in his arms.

Corey lay in Matt's arms, listening to his heart thunder in his chest, more confused than ever. Matt surprised her once more. He never let her make her little speech about how nice it had been and it should never happen again. He demonstrated, to Corey's complete satisfaction, that it could happen again. In fact, Corey never remembered feeling quite as content as she did this very minute. Her fears seemed groundless, insignificant when compared to the joy that Matt shared with her. Corey knew she wouldn't be able to resist him again. He had imprinted himself on her body, and Corey knew she would always respond to his touch.

Trying to keep it light, she teased him. "If this the hors d'oeuvre, I can't wait for the main course."

Matt pulled her closer to him, well aware she used humor when she was nervous or unsure of herself. "You are the entire feast, my beautiful Corey. And I plan on dining often."

Humor finally deserted her and she spoke straight from her heart. "Matt, what do you do to me? I've never felt like this before. I've never acted like this before."

"You've never had the right man before," Matt suggested, afraid to mention the love that he knew explained their behavior. If he told her he loved her, and suggested that she might love him, Corey would bolt from his bed—and maybe farther. *Slowly, Matthew Stone*, he told himself. *First she has to feel safe making love with you.*

"I've never felt anything like this before," Corey admitted quietly. "With anyone."

"Their loss, my sweet Corey. Don't you know how right we are together, how perfectly we match?"

Corey turned to Matt and looked into his eyes. "I don't know what to say. Mostly what you make me feel is confused. You were right, though. I did spend the day thinking of ways to tell you that this couldn't happen again. Now that seems so far away and so pointless."

"It'll be all right. Anything this wonderful can't be wrong."

"Maybe. But you know you don't really know much about me, not much more than I know about you. What we have," Corey decided as she struggled to find some sense of this basically out-of-control situation, "is a very strong chemical reaction to each other."

"What?" Matt asked her laughingly as he reached down and picked up the pillows that had been pushed accidently onto the floor. Propping them up behind his back, he pulled Corey to him, arranging her head on his shoulder. "Do you think that all this is because of our pheromones? That this is all some chemical attraction, that I want you because of the way you smell?"

"What else can it be? Falling in love means knowing everything about another person and liking them and admiring them. You know nothing about me. If you did, you'd feel differently," Corey said quietly, convincing herself as she spoke. "This is lust. That's all it can be. Pure unadulterated wonderful sex."

"You're such an expert you know the difference between lust and love, do you?" Matt asked before he realized that he was the only one who knew the difference. Corey didn't. The tender protectiveness that accompanied his sexual attraction to Corey, coupled with his deep appreciation of her intelligence, courage, and strength made him absolutely positive that love was what he was feeling. He hoped Corey felt the same. He also knew, even if she did return his feelings, she wasn't ready to label them as such or accept them as valid. He had no choice but to let her rationalize her own behavior—at least for now.

"Okay. For the benefit of your argument, let's assume that we have a strong chemical reaction to each other. What should we do about it?"

Nonplussed, Corey looked at him, her eyes widening. "I don't know. You're the expert here. How many women have you slept with? For all I know, I'm number four hundred and two, this month's model."

Matt answered Corey very carefully. "I won't deny I've had my share of women, although nowhere near as many as you imagine. Enough to know that this is very, very different. I care for you, whether you want me to or not. And you feel something for me or you wouldn't be so scared."

"I'm not scared, I'm just trying to work out the proper etiquette for this."

"Good. Then I think we've established that we want each other and that we are very good together." He stared at her until Corey was forced to nod her head. "Why don't we just take it one day at a time, as if we were any other couple? We can get to know each other with both our bodies and minds. If you're right, and I won't love you when I get to know you or that you won't be able to love me when you know me better, then we'll have had a wonderful, special affair. If I'm right, we'll find something more."

Corey lay still, trying unsuccessfully to find the flaw that she knew had to exist in Matt's logic. All she knew was that at this particular moment in time, the only place in the world she wanted to be was in Matt's arms. Corey was tempted to take a chance and let herself live for the present. She was no stranger to pain, and at least in this one case, she'd have known a golden pleasure before the darkness that was sure to follow.

"All right," Corey finally said as she slid her arms around his neck and brought her mouth to his.

"What do you mean, all right? All right to what?"

"Anything, everything. To whatever you want. An affair, I guess, until you leave. I can't resist you anymore. I've just discovered better loving through chemistry.'' With that quip, Corey pulled Matt back to her. It was another hour before they returned to reality.

When Corey heard Matt's stomach growl, so near to hers, she laughed, and pulled herself from his arms. "Let's go eat, dinner is quite late tonight, señor. I think we're operating on Spanish time, having our dinner at eleven.''

Pulling on robes, they walked downstairs, their hands clasped together. The spaghetti sauce had turned into something resembling putty and they were forced to chuck it. They scrounged in the refrigerator and made themselves a large tray of cold meats, cheeses, and fruit to eat in the living room. Corey discovered a bottle of sweet red wine in the back of her refrigerator and brought that out to accompany their dinner.

As they sat in front of the fire, warm and mellow, Matt casually asked Corey if she'd ever lived in Spain and really gotten used to eating dinner so late.

"I've been there, off and on over the years, but never long enough to adjust to their lifestyle. Years ago I was there for two months, but I was attached to a sheik's harem as a sort of combination liaison and bodyguard.''

"Were you really? Actually in the harem or whatever they call it? That has always fascinated me. As a professor involved in group dynamics, that is,'' Matt qualified as Corey raised her eyebrow. "It seems as though they're existing in a time warp, living about three hundred years out of tune. Are they truly happy?''

Corey thought for a moment and then shrugged. "I don't honestly know. Despite the western clothes they buy and their exposure to our movies and television, they seemed content to retain their insular lives. Maybe you have to consider that they're very well off and secure. And they're brainwashed from birth to believe that being a wife to a wealthy sheik is the highest honor that they would ever win. What about you?"

"I think my secretary friend had two wives, but we never discussed his personal life. As long as he kept giving me the needed documents and information, I was satisfied."

"Did you find any underlying threads in your research?"

"Surprisingly I did. You have to remember I'm only interested in the PF. How, where, and who gives them their financial backing. It's the money, as always, that leaves a trail. Perfect for someone with my background. I took my bachelor's in accounting, right down to being a CPA."

Corey listened intently, trying to integrate this new information. She knew that their conversation could lead in many different directions at this point. There was so much she wanted to learn about Matt. She wanted to know about the discoveries and dangers he had faced while researching his book. She wanted to know how and where he met his wife, she needed to know about his son. But, she found out, as she asked Matt her question, she most of all wanted to find out about the man himself.

"What happened to turn you from a CPA into a political scientist?"

"Damn, Corey, are you sure you want to hear about all that? It's a long story and all of it's old history."

Watching Matt unconsciously bring his right hand

to his brow and run his forefinger along his eyebrows, Corey realized that she had stumbled upon an important element of Matt's past. She noticed that gesture three other times, and all three times, Matt had been uncomfortable. When he didn't reply right away, Corey reached down, selected a red seedless grape and popped it into his mouth. "No big deal. You're entitled to your secrets, too."

Matt looked up. "No, it's not that. It's no secret. It's that I'm not particularly proud of that part of my life. Of all the things I want you to know about me, that's the one I'd pick last."

"Another time, then. This idea of knowing each other isn't carved in iron. We're lovers, not psychiatrists, after all."

Giving her a look of black irony, Matt leaned back and began talking. If he refused to tell Corey this, she would be justified in shutting him out of her past, too. "I was born and raised in a suburb of Philadelphia, thirty-five years ago. I'm the oldest of six kids. My father was an ambitious accountant, a hard working man, one with very strict standards and expectations. Accounting is his life, and he tried to make his children fit into his mold the way that numbers did, all neat and buttonholed in a safe category. I was to be the son who would take over the business. One of my sisters was to be a lawyer, another a doctor, etcetera. I think that I inherited his need for accuracy and precison, but, thank goodness, not his narrow view of the world."

Silently reaching for Corey's hand, he pulled her to him and then continued. "As the oldest, I was very conscious of my responsibilities. I lived up to his expectations all through college. I thought my life was all settled when I joined his firm, joined his entire life, the right clubs, everything. I was almost ready to marry the daughter of his partner when . . ." Pausing, Matt took a deep breath and poured himself another glass of wine.

"Forget it," Corey urged. "I didn't mean to get you upset when I asked about this. I don't want all this . . ."

"Well, you're going to get it. Maybe I don't like what I did, but it's a part of me, and I grew and learned from it. To make a long story short, my fiancée Susie got pregnant three months before the wedding. When I found out about it by accident, she told me I was one of three possible fathers. Before I had a chance to do anything, she had an abortion. I don't know, to this day, what I would have done if she'd kept the child. When she assumed that our wedding would go on as planned, I took a long hard look at me and my life, and I hated it. That's when I moved to California and went back to school."

"What was so bad that you didn't want to tell me? You weren't in the wrong, she was."

"It's not easy to admit I spent the first twenty-four years of my life living my father's dream. I'm ashamed I thought for even one minute that belonging to the right country club made any difference."

"You were too young to know any better, especially if you grew up in that environment. I'm more proud of you for changing your whole life. It took courage to do what you did, and I admire you for it. At twenty-four, I was still following orders without question. I didn't have my crisis of conscience until I was nearly twenty-nine. I was a lot slower than you."

"We've both done a lot of changing in our lives,

haven't we? And none of it easy," Matt murmured, tightening his grasp around her shoulders. "Shall we continue this discussion tomorrow? It's your turn to share some of your past with me."

"We'll see. I haven't agreed to play Twenty Questions, you know, just because you feel like telling me everything about your past."

"Okay, we'll play Ten Questions. I'll tell you more than you ever want to know about one Matthew James Stone, Ph.D., professor of political science, author, and mad passionate lover of one Corey . . ."

With a sigh, Corey supplied the name, "Winters."

"Corey Winters Hamilton," Matt finished with a smile. "Where did the Winters come from?"

"It was my grandfather's family name on my mother's side."

"Is that the grandfather who lived on the Cape and was a friend of Sean?"

"Yes. Grandpa Winters was probably the most important person in my life aside from my parents. He owned the only permanent home we ever had. Every summer we'd come and live with him, regardless where we were. Whenever Dad was overseas, Mom went with him and us kids came here to live. I think I probably lived more with my grandfather than with my own parents, all in all."

"What did he think of your becoming a spy?"

"He never knew. He died when I was fifteen, the year before I was approached." Sadly, she nestled closer to Matt's warmth. "I don't think he would have approved of it; he was old-fashioned and thought women belonged at home, or in 'feminine' jobs like teaching or nursing. He would have approved of the shop. He's the one who taught me to appreciate antiques and work on clocks. He and Sean. Sean was always around, and he sort of took over his role when Grandpa died. He's my last real family.''

"See . . ." Matt told Corey as he chucked her gently under the chin, "sharing isn't so hard. But it's almost one o'clock and we had better get to sleep.''

"Good grief. I didn't even get back to the Sanders house tonight. I'll have to go over tomorrow and really work hard to make up for this.''

"It's Monday tomorrow. Why not close the shop for the day and let me help you? We could probably do the rest of the house.''

"Why not? To be honest, if you weren't here, I would do exactly that. Close the shop and go do the inventory. I don't think it's very professional of me to let you come, though. You'd be safer here, with all the alarms.''

"I'll be safer with you than alone here, wouldn't I? Besides, no one traced us here. You said we'd be safe for a few days, that they wouldn't even be out looking for us yet.''

"What about your book?''

"I'm writing a section that requires some thought. The best thing I could do is get my mind off it for a few hours, let it mull around in my subconscious.'' Matt looked sincerely into her lovely blue eyes and hoped that she would accept that. He had no writer's block, nor any reason not to finish his book within the allotted time. Nonetheless, he was not going to leave Cape Cod until she agreed to become a part of his life, permanently.

Picking up the wine bottle and dirty dishes, Matt deposited them in the kitchen sink. When he returned, he found Corey poking the embers and closing the flue a notch. Tenderly he touched her shoulder and they got up together. By the time Matt returned from the bathroom, Corey was sound asleep in their bed.

Matt grinned as he stripped off his own clothes and followed her. Although Corey didn't know it, this would be the sleeping arrangement from now on. Matt had shared her bed for two nights now and wasn't about to let that prerogative change. Smiling into her tousled curls, Matt pulled her into his arms. With a sigh of contentment, Corey snuggled up to him, placing her head on his shoulder, smiling in her sleep.

TEN

The smell of coffee drifted up to Corey the next morning as she slowly opened her eyes. *What was she doing in her own bed?* she wondered fuzzily. As the soft pink sheets fell from her shoulders exposing her bare breasts, she sat up, suddenly wide-awake. The pillow beside her was still wrinkled and there was every evidence that she had spent the second night in a row sleeping with Matt.

As she adjusted the water in her shower, Corey realized that she had no right to be surprised. Last night she had agreed to have an affair with him. In a way, it was a relief to have the matter resolved. There had been a current of awareness between them since she opened the door on that first morning and found him in her doorway. At least the burning tension would be gone, and Corey would be able to handle Matt more easily now that he was satisfied. Soaping her body, she found that the thought of Matt's being satisfied turned her legs weak. "Satisfied" was a cool term to describe what Matt made her feel.

At least she now knew that she was capable of great sexual response. Chuck had been wrong calling

her frigid. It had been his cold, selfish lovemaking
that had been inadequate. Or perhaps, Corey realized
as she remembered a few of the things Chuck did that
should have thrilled her and hadn't, things that Matt
had done that made her melt, her unconscious mind
sensed that all Chuck's words had been lies, and was
unable to loosen its bonds on her body sufficiently to
allow her to find release with him. This time, her
body was sending her a vastly different message,
telling her that this man wasn't trying to hurt her.
This man felt right, touched right, loved right.

Drying off, Corey decided to stop thinking and
simply enjoy herself for once in her life. She knew
that it would hurt when Matt left her. She was one in
an endless string of women in his life since his wife
had died, but so what? It wasn't as if he was hiding
anything, or as if she didn't know that it was only
temporary. This could be a wonderful interlude for
them both.

Rummaging in her closet, Corey found a pair of
soft loden-green corduroy jeans. To match, she took
out one of her treasures, a sweater that she'd bought
three years ago in London. It was a special design,
made on the Isle of Wight, that was intricately knit-
ted and somberly beautiful. Although it contained at
least eight separate colors, all of them were muted
and soft to the eye as well as to the touch. The blues,
browns, greens, and grays blended into a geometric
pattern with two or three colors forming in a series of
patterns that swept around the sweater in wide cir-
cles, one blending into the other. It was beautiful and
warm, and one of Corey's most prized possessions.
As Matt's voice drifted up the stairs telling her breakfast was ready, she gave the woman in the mirror a
last glance. Even with no makeup, her complexion

glowed. Her love-swollen lips were a deep pink. Her eyes, however, were the real giveaway. They sparkled with life and vitality, and an eagerness to see her lover that all of Corey's training could not hide.

Matt stood at the stove listening for the sound of her footsteps on the stairs. This morning was important. He wanted to cement their relationship before Corey had a chance to change her mind again. When he saw her smiling face, he breathed a sigh of relief. It was going to be all right.

"Cream, no sugar?" Matt asked as he set the coffee on the table in front of her chair. "I hope you like scrambled eggs. That seems to be how my eggs usually turn out, no matter what I have in mind for them."

"Whatever you make is fine, Matt." She walked to the table and sat down, touched that he'd taken the time and effort to find her placemats and set the table. "You didn't have to go to this much trouble."

"I wanted to, love," Matt said easily as he walked up and set her coffee down in front of her. Bending down with the cup, he stooped to touch her lips with his, softly taking possession of what he already claimed. As she stirred beneath him, her lips automatically opening to his, Matt reluctantly moved back, lightly kissing her nose and forehead as he straightened up. "If I hadn't gotten right out of bed, with a stern purpose in my heart," Matt told her teasingly, "I would have jumped your bones, there and then, my lady, and we would have missed another meal." When he saw that Corey was smiling, he went on. "I know you have a deadline on the contents of that house and I aim to help."

"Okay," Corey said gratefully. He was going to

be casual, thank goodness, about this whole affair. If he had been too serious this morning, Corey didn't know what she'd have done. After the revelations of last night, she half feared Matt would start asking her questions about her past over breakfast. Questions that she couldn't answer, and not only because some of the information she knew was still classified as top secret. Matt wanted more of her than top secrets, she knew, but at least he was gentleman enough to postpone his probing for now.

"You can go with me under three conditions. One, you stay out of sight, indoors the entire time. Two, you stay within my view the entire time. Three, no questions about my past." She didn't mean to say that, it had slipped out, exposing her nervousness to him as clearly as a neon sign.

"Do I have to leave the door open when I go to the bathroom?" Matt teased. *Patience*, he told himself as he saw the muscles tense in her jaw. *She isn't ready for anything serious this morning, wouldn't answer any questions even if I were dumb enough to ask them.* It was enough, more than enough, that she agreed to sleep with him, that she was smiling when she first saw him this morning.

"You know what I mean. And if you want to leave the door open, fine with me. Nothing I haven't seen before."

Matt's leer at that statement made her turn, put her hands on her hips. "Don't you dare say what you're thinking."

"Who me? I was just glad that you're so concerned for my welfare," he returned, pleased with their banter.

"Seriously, professor, we are going to keep our personal life separated from our professional one. In the bedroom, our relationship is different than when I'm guarding you. I'm still in charge in that area,'' she insisted, welcoming the return of her professional objectivity. Thank goodness she hadn't entirely turned into a marshmallow by his presence. It would be all right. She was going to be able to keep the sex out of their everyday relationship, at least as long as he didn't touch her.

"I'll check the shop and grab my camera before we leave. I need pictures of the best items. I plan to be back here by early afternoon.''

"I trust you, Corey. Here, there, anywhere. You handled that situation in Boston like a pro.''

"I *am* a professional. Go and finish dressing.''

Grabbing her camera case, Corey walked to the back door and waited for Matt. She wouldn't think past the present. For once in her life, she would live for the day and worry about the future when it came.

"What kind of camera do you have?'' Matt asked as he came down fifteen minutes later. "Maybe I can take the pictures for you.''

"It's a 35mm Minolta. Do you think you can work with it?'' When Matt nodded, Corey handed him the camera, their fingers touching slightly as they moved the leather case from one to the other. Corey tensed when she felt herself reacting to that slight contact. Moving back, she gestured toward his hand. "There's extra film in the bottom of the case.''

"Let's do it. I'm ready to see the rest of your dream house in the daylight. How many bedrooms did you say it had?''

"Six, I think. Don't forget you'll need to get pictures of the attic and basement, too. This is our last trip over there and I want pictures of everything so I can finish up my appraisal in the shop." As she walked out the door, she reminded Matt to wait on the back porch until she drove the car around. "Same routine as usual."

"No problem, love," Matt told her, enjoying the play of emotions that the small endearment caused to flow over her face. If she realized how easily her emotions registered on her beautiful face, Corey would really have been disconcerted. Since the first time they'd made love, Matt found himself able to sense her mood by the slight changes on her face. He wasn't sure if she'd become more open or if he'd become so attuned to her every muscle that each small nuance became a neon sign. In truth, it was probably somewhere between the two.

Seeing the old house in full sunlight did nothing to lessen its appeal. "It's even more lovely in the daylight," he told her softly. "I can see how you fell in love with the place."

"It would be hard not to love this house. I just hope that a family buys it, not some corporation that wants to tear it down and put up a batch of condos."

"Do you know how much land goes with it?"

"I'm not sure, but I think it's around two acres."

"That shouldn't be large enough to attract any developers. Is it going on the market right away?"

"I don't know. I can't afford it one way or the other, so let's go and get this job finished. I hate you being so exposed."

"No one knows I'm even on the Cape, Corey. I don't know why you worry so."

"It's my job."

"I'll be all right." Hefting the camera, Matt got out of the car and walked around to the back door.

Corey locked the car and followed him up the steps. Once inside, Corey quickly went to work, anxious to finish the inventory but unable to hide her real excitement in the place.

Matt stood back and watched Corey for a moment. She was a woman of so many different moods and attitudes. This innocent joy was part discovery, he knew, but also part gladness that she might somehow help the old woman keep her home. There was not a trace of greed or self-interest in her, only a generosity of spirit that Matt knew was as rare as it was true. Suddenly he made the connection between Corey and his first wife, Sally.

It was simple, all too simple. They were both genuinely nice people, capable of a true, unswerving commitment, capable of unselfish love. Turning away for a moment, Matt fought the need to hold Corey, fought the need to take her there on that old quilt and force her to admit that they belonged together.

Playing devil's advocate, in an attempt to defuse his own emotion, he asked Corey, "Will you be able to afford any of these things?"

"Not much. Most of this stuff is museum quality."

"Then, will you get a finder's fee for all this work?"

"I suppose I'll be paid for the appraisal. I won't take anything more. You know this is a favor for Sean. Besides, I have enough for my needs."

Curious, Matt asked her, "You have money of your own, then?" He never asked her about money before. Or, for a matter of fact, told her that he was a rather wealthy man in his own right.

"I've got some money, more than enough for my needs now that Sean's taken care of. You know the government. Their benefits are better after you're retired. I more than break even at the shop. It's enough.''

"What did you mean, about Sean's being taken care of?"

Corey stood still for a moment, wondering what to tell him. She decided that after all they'd been through, Matt deserved the truth, or at least as much of it as possible.

"Remember when you first came here? My price for keeping you is my severance from the agency plus Parker's listing Sean on my medical insurance policy. I put him down as my 'family' a few years ago, in another bargain with Parker, in lieu of a raise. I kept my sick leave status with him because I couldn't afford for the policy to lapse. Sean's nursing home costs a bundle and his stroke pretty much cleaned him out.''

"You're something else, Corey Hamilton,'' Matt told her, touched by her loyalty and love for her godfather.

When she shrugged, Matt asked another question. "When did your father die?''

"Oh, five years ago, about. I was in Pakistan at the time,'' Corey answered as she absently got out her pad and stickers. "I'll always remember the day I was told he had died. It was summertime, and really hot. The entire country was shimmering in the heat, and I was sitting in a sweltering basement listening to some tapes of the Russian . . . a Russian. Anyway, my immediate sector boss came to tell me. Scared me to death, because no one was supposed to know where I was.

"It was ironic in a way. Dad was run down by a

drunk driver. After all the years as a pilot, after all the thousands of hours that Mom and I spent worrying about him flying, he got hit by a car. They told me I could go home for the funeral, but there wasn't any point. I would have been the only one there except Sean and Margie. And my job was very urgent right then. So I sent flowers, and Sean and Margie tended to the details. He would have understood. Duty always came first with him.''

Matt reached over to touch her shoulder in understanding, causing Corey to realize what she'd just told him.

"How did you get me talking about my past, Stone?'' Corey grumbled. "I swear you know a magic spell. I haven't talked this much about myself in years and years. So now you know one of my deep dark secrets. I didn't go to my own father's funeral. I still regret that, but there was no logical choice really.''

"No, Corey, there wasn't, or you would have done it. I'm sure he wouldn't have wanted you to do any different.''

"No, probably not,'' Corey agreed. "Look at the time,'' she mumbled as she caught sight of her watch. "We've got three hours to finish everything. Let's move it.''

Sitting in the backseat of Corey's blue Chevy four dusty, busy hours later, Matt's world shifted once again. Corey had left him in a secluded lot behind the local grocery as she ran in to pick up a few supplies on the way back to the shop. She was going to take Matt back first, but he convinced her that, for once, it wouldn't hurt if he was alone for fifteen minutes. She'd given him a newspaper, told him to stay behind it, and left.

"No!" Matt exclaimed out loud in an anguished tone, his eyes rapidly running back and forth over one of the items on the front page of the Boston newspaper he held. Ruffling the paper to find the back page that continued the headline story, Matt read it before impulsively getting out of the car. He strode to the phone booth that was no more than five feet from the car and quickly made a call. Four minutes later he was back in the car, his expression set and worried.

Corey found him rigidly sitting in the car when she returned. As soon as she got in, Matt held up the newspaper. "Did you see this?"

"See what?" Corey asked him as she started the engine.

"The paper."

"I haven't read it, if that's what you mean. I didn't even notice the headlines before I handed it to you. Did something happen in the Mideast? I confess I haven't paid a lot of attention to world news since you got here."

"Ten people were shot and robbed at Bartollini's Restaurant in Boston last night, and four of them are in critical condition. Four masked gunmen entered the premises at eight o'clock, robbed the patrons of all their jewelry and wallets and then, at random, shot several of them," he explained cursing fluently. "No reason."

"That's horrible." Looking sideways, she noticed that his normally bronzed face had paled and that his hands were tightly gripped on the newspaper as he scanned an inside follow-up column for more details. "What's wrong? Why are you so disturbed by this incident? Not that it isn't tragic."

"One of my oldest and best friends was one of the

victims. 'Harry Farmer,' '' Matt read aloud in a shaken voice, " 'distinguished member of Harvard's political science department, was one of the people injured in the incident. He was rushed, with six of the other victims, to Boston General Hospital late last night. Farmer and his dinner companion, an unidentified woman in her early twenties, were rushed into surgery and are both said to be in critical condition.' '' Taking a deep breath, he started to tell Corey that he'd called the hospital switchboard but had not been able to get any information beyond the fact that Harry was still alive.

"I'll call Parker and have him find out how your friend is."

"Why not call the hospital?"

"You know hospitals, they never give out much information," Corey said carefully, not wanting Matt to know that her suspicious mind was immediately wondering if there might be some connection between the incident and the people looking for Matt. "I'll get Parker to talk to the doctors personally. We can have a full rundown on your friend's condition."

Unless Corey knew for sure, she refused to let Matt even suspect that he might be the hidden cause of any more violence. He already felt guilty enough about losing his wife and son to terrorists. There was no need for him to suffer needlessly thinking he might be the cause, even indirectly, for the shooting of ten more people. Corey knew better than anyone what a burden innocent lives were on one's conscience. The odds were high that it was an unrelated incident. That restaurant, despite its excellent food, was notorious for being a hangout of the Boston underworld. Still, in her line of work, any coincidence could never be overlooked.

Minutes later, Corey faced Matt with a determined look in her eye. "He's lunching with the secretary of state and isn't to be disturbed unless it's an emergency." Pausing, Corey added, "As much as you care about Harry, you have to agree it is not an emergency. I'll call Parker again at two."

"Thanks. I know there's nothing I can do from here, but I do want to know. I really hate all this hiding and secrecy. A lot of the time it seems unreal, like a James Bond movie or something. Some days I expect to hear a guy in the distance calling, 'It's a take.' Then we could walk out of here, free and clear."

"I know this isn't easy for you," Corey said carefully. *So all of this seems like a movie to him, does it?* Corey couldn't help but wonder if he meant her, too. Was she the blond actress that came with the script and was just as disposable when the director called, "wrap it up?" Unfortunately, Corey would bet money that this was the case as she reminded herself that she'd gone into this affair with full knowledge, knowing it would end when Matt finished his book.

"So . . ." Corey said briskly, putting away the contents of the brown shopping bags, "I'll finish this and you head upstairs and get to work. I'll let you know as soon as I find out anything about Harry. Writing is the best thing you can do now. As soon as you're done with the book, you'll be able to go in and visit your friend personally."

"I think you're right, I'll get going. I'm on chapter eleven and should be finished in a couple of weeks, if I hurry. Are you up for reading the first ten chapters tonight?"

"Sure, Matt. Anything I can do to help. All part

of the service," Corey quipped, trying to sound cheery but succeeding only in striking a brittle note that got Matt's attention.

"What did you mean by that?"

"Nothing special," she said. "I want to help you, that's all, so that you'll be able to get back to your regular life."

Matt stalked over to grab her shoulders and spun her to face him. "Don't go playing games with us, Corey. I didn't mean that I want to be free of you, and I won't let you start sniping. When I said I was tired of hiding, I meant that, and only that. What I want most in the world, my reluctant love, is to take you out in the open and tell the whole world that you are my woman. I want to take out a newspaper ad stating that Corey Hamilton belongs with Matthew Stone. I want all that, and more. The end of my book is going to be a beginning for us, Corey, just a beginning."

"Go and write, Matt," Corey said in a choked voice. "I'll open up for the rest of the afternoon." As she did, she wondered if Matt spoke the truth. Maybe he meant it and maybe he didn't. Either way, it didn't matter. When his book was finished, he would go back to his life in California and Corey would have to think about her own future. She wasn't going to argue with him now. There was no point in spoiling their remaining time with petty disagreements that had no solution.

The afternoon passed quickly for Corey. She finally got Parker and extracted a promise from him that he'd get a full report from the hospital and let them know. When he called back with the news that Farmer was still in intensive care, Corey dutifully passed the news to Matt, along with Parker's promise that he'd call when the injured man's condition changed.

Finally she put in a call to Sean, anxious to share her good news with her old friend. At first he thought she was exaggerating until Corey actually listed some of the pieces she'd found and photographed. After a few minutes, Corey hung up with her friend feeling good. At least some things turned out better than expected. Mrs. Sanders' financial worries were over.

Matt was quiet and preoccupied during dinner. Corey knew he was still deeply concerned over his friend and she was filled with tenderness. Handing him a glass of after-dinner brandy, Corey led him over to the fireplace and pushed him onto the soft cushions of her sofa. "Why don't you tell me what you're thinking? Maybe it'll help if you talk about it."

"I don't know," Matt muttered, drawing his finger over his eyebrows in the familiar gesture that Corey had come to cherish. "I just keep wondering if he's going to be all right."

"Parker said Harry's holding his own. That's the best we can expect. We'll hear more tomorrow."

"I know. I'm sorry I haven't been better company tonight."

"You don't have to entertain me, for Pete's sake." Reaching over, Corey put her arms around Matt's shoulders and pulled him close to her. "I . . . I want to help if I can, that's all."

"You help just by being here." Leaning back, he held the brandy glass in his hand, swirling the warm liquid. With a sigh, he began to share his memories about Harry, telling Corey of their first meeting and the ups and downs they shared during their years of graduate school.

"You and Harry really did that?" Corey asked, through a mass of near-hysterical giggles. "You guys really filled that guy's whole apartment with crumpled newspaper while he was on his honeymoon?"

"Silly, wasn't it, but I did enjoy that time. I think I had a delayed adolescence or something. Harry and I were like kids that first year, away from home for the first time. There I was, twenty-four years old and finding out that I really wasn't a stuffy accountant after all. It was a good time, Corey. I wish you'd been there."

"I would have been nineteen, and not at all your type. Wasn't that where you met Sally?" Corey asked in a small voice. She knew that Matt had been thinking about his wife, had in fact been editing some of the stories that he'd told her about Harry. "Wasn't she with you during a lot of those adventures?"

"Yeah, she was. She and Harry and I were together a lot the last two years I spent at UCLA."

When Matt fell silent, Corey sighed and leaned over to him.

"It's all right to remember, Matt," she told him softly. "It's all right to talk about her, too. She was a huge part of your life and . . . I don't want you to ever, ever feel you have to pretend in front of me."

Wanting to say more, wanting to hear less, Corey fell silent. She was afraid, at that moment, that she might love Matt, might be making a commitment in her heart that would lead to nothing but pain. She told herself not to sit there, encouraging the man she loved . . . no, *her lover* to tell her about his dead wife. *You don't want to hear about how perfect she was and how you'll never be able to replace her. You don't need any more grief. Remember, he's going out of your life in two more weeks. Cherish the memories you can make but don't let yourself ever hope for more.*

Before Matt could speak, Corey leaned over to place a tender kiss on his lips. "Take me to bed and make us more memories," she whispered. "Memories for a cold winter's night."

"Corey, my love," Matt answered before her tongue invaded his mouth, before her hands moved up and down his long legs and set his body on fire. "Later, we'll talk later," he agreed before they came together, slipping to the hard floor in front of the fire.

If Corey's lovemaking was desperate, so was Matt's. If Corey's need to touch and be touched was too urgent for words, so was his. Together they burned like tinder, hot and fast. Their clothing slipped from them as though by magic, his shirt sliding off under her seeking hands, her mouth covering his warm chest with small licks, as though she were memorizing him with her teeth and tongue. Her jeans slid off, and soon they were both undressed, flesh touching flesh, burning, igniting. Corey pushed Matt back on the floor and gazed at her lover with need, wanting to memorize his body, to take all of him into her, to become one with him.

Together they shared and explored, urgently claiming the other in every way. Finally, their desire burned so hot, their need for total union became so great that they could stay apart no more. Matt lay on his back, pulling Corey over him. Matt looked up, seeing Corey's eyes closed in passion, her face drawn tight with need, and knew at that moment that he'd never loved like this before, and that this woman was his for now and evermore.

Heat and need and mindless joy filled Corey as she moved with Matt. Suddenly, his strong hands grasped her hips, holding her motionless while he surged into her, driving them both into a starburst of feeling that etched itself into very cell of Corey's memory. Never, never had she felt like this, felt a molten glow that filled and enticed her very soul. Matt satisfied all of her, in every way, in every dark corner.

Contented, she lay on his broad chest, their slick skins touching. Only opening her eyes when he'd moved from her, she allowed him to pull her up and they soundlessly climbed up the stairs to her warm bed. Corey whispered, "My love," to Matt as he tucked her beside him, unaware that she'd given him a gift more precious than diamonds.

Several hours later, Corey awoke, apprehension spreading through her. Sitting up, she heard the unmistakable sound of the back-door alarms being de-activated, the three beeps that turned her blood to icewater. "No, no, he wouldn't be such a fool," Corey hissed as she ran from the bedroom to look out her window. Glancing at the clock on her dresser, Corey saw that it was just past seven A.M., still dark and foggy as night, but, Corey thought, late enough for a hospital switchboard to be open. Grabbing the first item of clothing she could reach, Corey struggled into a pair of jeans as she saw the top of Matt's dark head descend the first step of her back porch.

She left the room, clad only in the jeans, stopping only long enough to jam her feet into a pair of boots that had been left in the front of her closet. She reached the back door in time to see Matt start to circle around the house. She wasted a good minute in the hall closet, groping for any sort of jacket to cover her bare breasts. In a dead run, she set off after him, sure that she'd catch up with him and find out just where the idiot thought he was going alone in the dark.

Corey was almost close enough to shout his name when it happened. Matt was stepping into the phone booth on the corner, his face illuminated in the dim glow of the streetlight that shone on the corner. Two huge men came from the shadows and simply grabbed him. Efficiently, one stuck a blanket over his head while the other lifted his feet and they simply pushed him into the backseat of a car that pulled up. Corey began running in earnest, but they sped away before she could close the distance to the car. If she'd had her gun she would have shot out the tires. All she could do was memorize the license plate number. It was all over in one minute, a very professional job. As smooth as she'd ever seen, and she had seen one too many.

Frozen for a moment, Corey hesitated as she blinked to retain her consciousness. For a second she actually imagined she was going to faint for the very first time in her life. The professional in her came back in that moment, and the woman who was within hid behind a block of ice, not thinking, not *wanting* to think about what happened.

Slapping her pocket, she was thankful to find change, and she ran into that phone booth and had Parker on the line in two or three long minutes. "Parker, block off the Cape. They got Matt about three minutes ago. A black Lincoln with a Mass. license plate," Corey told him, rattling off the number. "There were three men, and all very good."

Holding the line, Corey forced herself to think logically. It must have something to do with Matt's friend. That unmitigated fool must have called the hospital himself to check on his friend and not told her. It was the only explanation that made any sense. Otherwise, why sneak off in the morning like this to a phone booth? She was going to kill him, if and when they ever saw each other again, Corey promised herself.

ELEVEN

Unbelievable as it seemed to Cory, the men who were after Matt must have created the whole incident in Boston solely to find him. People that desperate would stop at nothing, she knew, but the shooting of ten people in a restaurant just on the chance of flushing out one person was unbelievable. Still, men capable of blowing up airplanes and buses full of helpless people wouldn't balk at shooting a paltry number like ten.

"Corey . . ." Parker's voice came through. "The road block will be in place in minutes, but we don't know if they'll try to get him off the Cape in a boat, or whatever. I'll have the license number traced in a few minutes. Tell me what happened. How did they find you?"

There was a moment of silence when Corey finished telling Parker the whole story, down to her speculation that the shooting incident in Boston was staged to find Matt. "If that's the case, we have a good chance of finding him. Stone couldn't have been stupid enough to give his name, so they must be checking out everyone who called in about Farmer's condition. Your phone booth can't have been their only target. I'm betting that they've got him hidden somewhere on the Cape, waiting for a superior to get there.''

While Corey waited, Parker shouted orders to his assistants. ''Did they see you?'' he then asked Cory. ''Do you think they know that we got their license number? Think.''

''No, they never saw me. It was too dark and I wasn't close enough to make any noise.''

''Better and better. They know that Matt was somewhere in the area then, but they don't know exactly where. All right. I'm sending everyone in Boston out to help you, Corey. Go back to your shop and wait. Hanks and Kelly should be there in minutes. We've already called them. Are his papers safe? That information must be sheer dynamite. I have never seen an operation of this scale in the United States before. They must have tapped the hospital switchboard. Think of the equipment they needed for that. And the manpower. I have to admit that I was way off this time. The Israelis were right on target. I should have pulled Stone after Boston.'' Clearing his throat, Parker added, ''I'll call you if we hear anything.''

''No. I can't just sit still and wait, Parker. I can't.'' When her voice took on a high note, Corey abruptly fell silent, struggling to maintain her composure. ''I'll take a run through some of the smaller places that rent cabins by the week or month. You won't be able to start checking on them until nine o'clock when the real estate offices start opening up.''

''All right, but only after Hanks and Kelly get there to guard the store and we secure his papers. Then you can go and look. Only promise me, if you find him, you call in. These guys are armed and dangerous.'' Parker hesitated for a moment, then added, "Don't blame yourself. Stone should have known better."

When Corey didn't reply, Parker continued. "Don't worry. We have the edge. They won't kill him until they get the manuscript. And that means they'll come to the shop before anything happens. We'll get them."

Corey hung up the phone with that thought echoing through her mind. She knew what it implied, and the thought of it burned deep within. They would be able to make Matt talk, she knew for sure. The methods she didn't want to think of. . . . She couldn't allow herself to think of. She only hoped Matt wasn't stupid enough to try being brave. It wouldn't do him any good in the long run.

Thirty minutes later, she was calmly getting into her car. Hanks was in her back room, while Kelly watched the shop from the outside. A complete copy of Matt's notes and manuscript had been slipped into an envelope, and Corey's first stop was the post office where she sent them, express mail, to Washington. After that, she began to drive slowly along the coast, using every bit of control that she possessed.

For the second time in a month, she was glad of her training, glad that she could do something to help, anything. If she'd had to sit waiting back at the store, she would have gone mad. This way, at least she was moving, looking for anything that might hint of the unexpected visitors. She forced herself to think logically, to put herself in their position. They wouldn't know the Cape, she decided, and would try to stay close to the one major road that ran through this part of the Cape back toward Boston.

For the umpteenth time, Corey once again glanced down at her watch. It was ten o'clock, fully three hours since Matt had been taken. Three of the longest hours in Corey's life. Her internal clock ticked relentlessly as she struggled to maintain the rigorous discipline of her years on the job. "Be cool and professional or he'll die. Use your brain not your emotions," she repeated to herself over and over again. But the knowledge that it was Matt out there, her Matt, not some impersonal subject, made the discipline a form of torture that she never wanted to repeat.

Corey had been slowly, patiently weaving her way back toward Boston. She was going five miles on either side of the major highway, driving down every little street and lane, scanning for the black Lincoln, watching for anything out of the ordinary that might signal Matt's presence.

Sensing something amiss, Corey braked to a stop in the middle of the block. She tried to pinpoint what in particular had caught her attention. It hadn't been the black car—she would have noticed that outright. Covering her face with her hands, she forced herself to recall what it was that had triggered the warning bells in her head. When she closed her eyes, all she could see was Matt gazing at her in accusation. "I will not let them hurt you," Corey promised the image in her mind.

A window, that was it. There was a small cottage set back from the road that had not one but two broken windows. It wasn't an old or abandoned dwelling, either, but one that was nicely cared for, with flowers and nicely trimmed shrubs framing its newly painted shutters. The broken windows weren't boarded up, either, only covered with newspaper. It was something definitely out of the ordinary and worth checking.

Corey turned the car off, and then reached down to

check that her gun was securely in place in her boot before softly closing the car door. She took the key off its key ring and slipped it firmly in her right front pocket and shoved her purse under the seat. She didn't lock the doors, in case this was the right place and she needed a quick exit. Fading back into the trees that bordered the back of the street, she began to silently move toward the cottage.

Matt stirred briefly as he came to consciousness, lying still as the throbbing of his limbs told him that something was wrong. Every bone in his body ached, and he was lying on the floor. With a start, he remembered what had happened last night and began to curse himself.

When he made a mess of things, he did it royally. He was a bloody fool. No doubt about it. It was all his fault, all of it. Worse, he knew that Corey would be suffering for his mistake, blaming herself for his capture. She had an amazing ability to take on guilt, even if it didn't belong to her. He had to escape, as much for her as for himself. There would be enough time for recriminations and regrets later. At the moment he needed to find out how bad a mess he was in.

Forcing his eyes open, he saw that he was lying next to the door of a cheerful little room with white walls, a blue carpet, and red gingham curtains and bedspread. It was still daylight, and he wondered how long he'd been unconscious.

He must still be on the Cape, Matt decided, unless they'd moved him while he was out. His kidnappers had driven only fifteen or so minutes from the time they first put the blanket over his head until they forced him out of the car and into a building. He knew he'd fought them, remembering the sound of broken glass when he thrashed around as soon as he set foot inside the door. Then everything went blank.

The good thing was that he was alone—the bad that his hands and feet were tied, but thankfully in the front so that the circulation wasn't totally gone. Suppressing a groan, he moved his wrists so that he could see his watch. It was almost ten o'clock, three hours since he'd been snatched. Obviously he'd been hit in the head, but other than that, he seemed to be in one piece.

As he recalled the conversation he'd overheard in the car, Matt drew a deep breath of relief. The goons who picked him up had no idea of where he was staying. Corey was safe for the time being. Someone was coming from Boston to interrogate him properly. He'd heard that much in the car. Two of his captors had been speaking in Arabic, unaware that he understood them. They had rejoiced that they'd been the ones to find him and were planning to call their superior as soon as they had Matt put away. When their boss came, the American would tell them everything they wanted to know, including the location of his hideout. Then they would be rewarded for their good work.

Not if he could help it! He had to escape and do it now. The bonds on his wrists didn't look very encouraging. They'd used a very thin nylon rope and knotted it well. His ankles were in no better condition. After a frustrating minute of tugging and pulling with his teeth, he realized it was impossible.

The most logical thing to do was to get himself to the window and open it. If he could, he'd shout for help from a passerby. Until someone came by, he'd see if he could break a light bulb or something and try to cut himself free.

Carefully, he used his feet to push himself up the nearest wall. He edged up, willing himself to be quiet. After inching his way over, he started to open the window when he saw movement in the woods behind the house. Peering out, he spotted Corey approaching the house. She had somehow found him. All he had to do was attract her attention.

As Corey looked up at the small cottage, she wondered why she felt so anxious. This was not the first house she'd checked out that morning, but it was the most promising. Most likely it was a lazy homeowner who was planning to fix his windows later. Except a conscientious homeowner didn't normally break both a front and side window in a house and then leave them, covered only with newspapers, through the cool damp Massachusetts night. And, how in the world could anyone have managed to break and cover two separate windows before ten in the morning? It would be like Matt to struggle, if he could, and that would account for the two broken windows.

Suddenly she stopped, the flickering of a curtain on the top floor getting her attention. She melted back into the trees and gazed up to the window. Red-and-white checks fluttered, revealing a man's face. Matt!

Waves of relief streamed through her body, making her momentarily weak. Leaning back against a tree, she took a deep breath and told herself that it wasn't over yet. She still had to get him out of the house and safely away. Her heart, however, seemed only concerned with one thing. He was still alive. Not until that very instant did Corey realize that she feared he was already dead, that she'd been so afraid

NO HIDING PLACE / 181

of that possibility that she not once allowed it to enter
her mind.

She was just turning to go and call Parker when
she heard the faint growl of a powerful engine and
saw a large black car coming down the street. There
was not time for backup. She had to get Matt out of
there now.

Taking a chance that the captors would be occupied with their visitors, Corey ran to the back of the
house and shimmied up a drainpipe that ran beside
the window to the roof. Carefully, she shifted one leg
over the windowsill and moved into the room. Taking in his tied hands and feet in a single glance, she
paused a second to run her hand down his cheek. She
reached down to her left boot and took out a knife
that made short work of the nylon twine that held
Matt's feet and hands together.

"Are you okay?" Corey whispered. "There is
another car just arriving and we better get out of here
now. Can you walk?"

Matt nodded in the affirmative while rubbing his
hands together and taking a few steps to restore his
circulation.

"Can you go down that drainpipe or would you
rather lower yourself down from the ledge and jump
the rest of the way?"

Before Matt could answer her, they both heard a
voice in the hall and froze. Corey motioned Matt to
lie down while she moved to behind the door. Without questioning, Matt obeyed her.

The door opened and a swarthy man walked in,
looking down at the floor. Corey immediately put her
gun to his ear, cocking the trigger so that he could
hear it. She closed the door behind him, pulling his

arm behind his back. In Arabic she whispered for him to be quiet or die on the spot.

After removing his gun and forcing him to his knees, Corey remained behind the man. Her gun did not move from its resting place behind his ear. "Now call down and tell them that the man is still unconscious and that you will bring him down in a few minutes, as soon as you awaken him."

When the dark man hesitated a moment, Corey put her other hand across the man's windpipe, fingers resting on the pressure points behind the ear. Briefly she closed her hand, causing the man to grunt in pain. As Matt rose to his feet, she motioned to him to use his belt to tie the man's hands behind him.

"Last chance," Corey whispered in Arabic as Matt finished. Matt quickly picked up the terrorist's gun and slid it in his waistband as he watched Corey and her captive. "Hand me a pillow," Corey ordered, not taking her eyes from the man. "It'll muffle the shot."

At that, the terrorist nodded and Corey released a little of her pressure on his neck. "One false word and it will be your last," she warned in his language.

The man complied with her order, his voice hoarse from the pressure of her hand. He shouted down that he'd be a couple of minutes. Before he could say anything more, Corey clipped him on the back of the neck with her gun and let him slide to the floor. She put a chair under the doorknob and moved rapidly over to the window.

"Now, ease down and let yourself drop to the ground. Move toward the trees and run to the right. The car's one block down."

Within a minute, they were both on the ground. Grabbing his hand, she took off at a dead run toward the shelter of the trees and then down the street toward their car. Matt stumbled because of the poor circulation in his leg, but Corey pulled him along until they reached the relative safety of Corey's station wagon.

"Did you see how many men were in the house?" Corey asked as she gazed over her shoulder while retrieving the key from her pocket.

"I never actually saw anyone, just heard their voices. They didn't know that I could speak Arabic fluently so they were pretty frank when they spoke. I think there were three of them, watching that phone booth. They were going to call their boss as soon as we were safely in the house."

Just as Corey turned the key to start her car, four men burst out of the cottage and jumped into the two cars. Three others ran into the woods behind the house and fanned out, one heading up the street toward them. Corey started her engine and took off, knowing that the terrorists would be after any car that moved. There wasn't much choice, however, as the one on foot would be able to see into her car any moment and he would shout a warning that would bring the rest. She concentrated on her driving, knowing that they would be safe in just a few miles.

"Take the gun, and see if you can get their tires," Corey ordered as she drove down the narrow wooded road that would lead into the turnpike in three miles, a car coming up rapidly behind her. "We'll be fine if we can get to the main road. There's a roadblock every two or three miles."

"They're gaining on us," Matt shouted as he turned on the seat and rolled down his window. "Try to drive straight a moment," Matt added, releasing the safety on the terrorist's pistol. She was pleased when

she saw Matt holding the gun comfortably and carefully aiming. The car pulled back when Matt fired,
but didn't stop. Immediately they returned fire, and
Corey began swerving wildly to avoid their bullets.
"Down," she shouted as she floored her powerful
car.

Finally Corey got to the main highway and turned
onto it, with the black Lincoln in full pursuit. She put
her foot down to the floor and moved away from the
larger car, speeding down the near-empty road. Corey
breathed a sigh of relief a couple of minutes later
when they rushed past a pair of police cars positioned
next to the highway.

The two patrol cars joined in the chase, their sirens
screaming. As she expected, the Lincoln pulled off
and left them, turning over the grass median and
reversing direction. One of the police cars followed
them, the other went on after Corey.

She immediately slowed down and yelled at Matt
to drop the gun over the side of the car and slowly
put his arms up. "Don't get them upset," she warned
as he complied and dropped the gun.

"We did it, Matt," she whispered, as the police
walked up to the car. "You're safe."

"Officers . . ." Corey began as the first policeman walked up slowly behind their car, guns drawn.
She put her hands in the air and started explaining.
"I'm Corey Hamilton and this is the Matthew Stone
you're looking for. I'll get out of the car very slowly,
and let you get my ID." Turning around, she told
Matt to do the same thing, reminding him to make no
quick moves.

Slowly Corey got out of the car and leaned over to
relax her hands on the roof. She told the officer that
her ID was in her left pocket and let him take it out

himself. "I've never been so glad to see you guys in my life," she said.

In a couple of seconds, the police had lowered their guns.

"Let me use your radio, please, and I'll call my boss and give him the address of the house they used. I imagine they're gone by now, but it's worth checking out."

Instead, the older of the two patrolmen went to call in the warnings while the other stood, staring at Corey. "Are you really a government agent?" he asked in awe. "You look more like a model or actress."

Matt walked around the car in time to hear that question, and he smiled down at Corey as he placed a long arm around her now trembling shoulder. "I can vouch for her," Matt told the young man. "She's a bona fide agent all right, down to the knife in her boot and training in karate."

Relief had made him giddy. It had not done so with Corey but had added a snap to her voice that normally didn't exist. She felt as though she'd been shattered into a million pieces and put back together again, but not in the same order. "I'm an ex-agent, Stone, if you want to get technical. And I don't have a black belt, only some very specialized training."

Briefly Corey wondered what Matt thought of her now, after seeing that scene with the terrorist. She had not seemed very feminine, with her gun pointing in the man's neck and a chokehold over his throat. Idly she wondered if Matt realized that she'd been serious. At that point, she would have killed that man, done anything to rescue him. Closing her eyes for a moment, she cleared her mind. Right now, Matt was all that mattered.

The policeman looked slightly skeptical. "Really?" he asked her.

"Some women can take care of themselves, sergeant," Corey replied before she swiveled in Matt's arms. "Are you all right?" she asked him. "Did they hurt you?"

"No, only my pride. Being carried around like a sack of potatoes isn't good on the ego. They banged me on the head, nothing more. They were waiting for their boss to come, and I don't think he was planning on asking me nicely. You arrived in the nick of time. How did you ever find me?" Leaning down, he placed a tender kiss on her nose. "Thank you, my love."

As the policeman watched with interest, his partner came back and faced them both. "All taken care of. A Mr. Parker wants to meet you back at your place, miss. We're supposed to follow you there."

"Thanks," Corey said. "Don't worry, I'm not planning any quick maneuvers. Today there's nothing I want to see more than your flashing blue lights in my rear window." Turning, she motioned to Matt to get back in their car. "You better get your story together. I'm willing to bet Parker is waiting for us and neither one of us has much good to say for ourselves. What happened?"

"I called the hospital when I read the paper yesterday. And I tried to again this morning. I'm the fool who rushed out alone. I'm the one who didn't follow your orders."

"There's no excuse for me. None whatsoever. I should have guessed you'd call by yourself. I was the idiot who let you out of the house. I was in charge, and I should have protected you. I even suspected that they'd shot Harry to bring you to the surface and didn't say so because I didn't want you to feel guilty. If I'd warned you, maybe you wouldn't have called. "I almost got you killed," she added quietly.

"Bull," Matt thundered. "I won't have you taking the blame for my stupid behavior. *I* was the one who called. In a way, you saved me. If I hadn't been so affected by your security, lady, I'd have called from the store and then we would both be dead. I heard the men curse me for using the phone booth. That was all that kept me alive for you to rescue."

Their discussion was temporarily suspended as they pulled in front of the store. There were four official government vehicles parked in front of the shop, a helicopter on the beach, as well as the two patrol cars that had followed Corey home and were now parked in her back driveway. "It looks like Parker's here."

As Corey walked up the step, the door flew open and Parker himself pulled her into the living room. "Good work, Corey. I see you found our wandering author without any help from me or my men. How many times do I have to tell you, call in when you need help," he asked, pursing his lips.

"There wasn't time, Parker. I found Matt just seconds before the interrogators pulled up. A quick exit was strongly indicated. I wouldn't have vouched for Matt's safety for even ten more minutes."

They were both debriefed by Parker for the next hour, with Matt slowly and patiently repeating all of the conversation that he'd overheard. Finally, the government man left them alone sitting on the sofa before the fireplace while he made use of the phone in Corey's office.

"So, tell me why you called from the damn phone booth this morning? I already found out about Harry!"

"Put it down to stupidity. Just plain stupidity. And

a lack of trust,'' Matt admitted, hastening to continue. ''Not in you, Corey, but in Parker. I wanted to know if Harry was really alive. I figured Parker was perfectly capable of letting me miss Harry's funeral for security reasons, and I refused to read about the death of my best friend in a damn obituary column days later.

''Besides, I find it hard to let you control everything,'' he added, staring straight ahead, his hands clasped on his knees. ''I know it's not very liberated, but part of me wants to be the one who makes the decisions. It's always been hard for me to follow orders. Can you forgive me?'' he asked, turning back to her and threading his long fingers through her hair. ''I always seem to be apologizing to you. I promise I'll obey all your orders from now on.''

''You're the one who almost got killed, not me. I know it's hard for you, but I can't change who I am. Even if I wanted to,'' Corey whispered, as much to herself as to him. She'd known all along it wouldn't work, it couldn't work. A strong man like Matt was bound to resent her for so many reasons, would be bound to detest her if he ever found out all of her past. He would be distressed at her capacity for violence once he thought through what'd happened that day. Right now he was glad to be safe, but sooner or later he'd look at her, remembering her fingers on the gun and wonder what sort of woman she was.

This was the end. Better to be done with it now. He was alive, and unhurt, though due to no great skill on her part. She had to let him go now, before she grew any weaker and revealed her feelings for him. Or admitted them to herself.

Straightening up, Corey gently removed his hands

from his face and took them into her lap. "I don't know what will happen. One thing I'm sure of, you'll have to be moved. You can't stay here anymore. Even if they haven't pinpointed our location, it will only be a matter of hours before they do."

"What? Move?" He hadn't thought that far into the future.

"You heard me, I'm sure they'll move you to another safe house. I'm hopelessly compromised now. Lucky I don't plan on doing this anymore." After this fiasco, Parker would probably be relieved that she wasn't an agent anymore. Never in all her ten years of work had she been so sloppy. She should never have let him out of the house, never have let him out of her sight, never have fallen asleep in his arms. Then again, never in her ten years had she cared so deeply about her subject that all her professional judgment was compromised. Better for them all to part company. She couldn't trust herself with Matt's safety any longer.

TWELVE

"I'm not going anywhere without you," Matt stated, cold fear drifting up his back. If he left Corey now, he wasn't sure that he would ever get her back. He needed more time. Once she slipped away, there would be too much time for her to convince herself that she wasn't right for him. "Our deal was that you guard me until the book is finished. It's not finished and I'm not going to let you break your word."

"Be reasonable, Stone," Parker said as he entered the room behind him, hearing the last sentence that Matt uttered. "She's right, you've got to move. It was bad enough when they found out you were in the Boston area. This is impossible."

"Didn't you capture them? I can't believe they got away again."

Patiently, Parker reminded Stone of the facts as he and Corey exchanged looks of unvented frustration. "Sure we caught them. Just like we caught the men in Boston. Don't you recall the little nicety that we call diplomatic immunity, Professor Stone? All we can do is deport them, that's it. We were lucky this time, though. Two of them were in the country as students. When they took a couple of shots at the police, they were arrested. They'll go to jail, but not the rest. You know the rules. The main point is that they know where you are. You're going to have to move."

"Only if Corey goes with me."

Parker frowned, wondering what to say. Corey was definitely involved, even if it seemed more personal than professional. Still, she was using her skills, and after today's incident, she might find she was willing to come back to work. When the silence stretched past two minutes, Parker cleared his throat and made a suggestion. "I have access to a condominium on the riverfront in Mystic, Connecticut. There's one recuperating agent there already. He and Corey should be capable of guarding you. Assuming you've learned your lesson, Stone."

"Will you go with me, Corey?" Matt asked, his eyes openly vulnerable and wanting. "You promised to stay with me till the book is finished. Besides, you haven't finished editing it." With an oddly hesitant voice, he leaned down to whisper in Corey's ear. "Please, love. I need you."

She looked up into his dark-blue eyes and saw the need, and the honesty. "What about my shop? And I'm not done with the appraisal for the Sanders house," Corey argued, knowing she should not go, afraid that she would never be able to leave him if she didn't do it now.

Clearing his throat, Parker interfered. "You did promise to see this thing through to the end, Corey." If Stone wasn't happy, he'd never get the book done. After all this, Parker suspected that Stone's book was even more important than he at first realized. "You wouldn't be safe until Matt's book is done, anyway. They've got your license plate and probably know where you live. Think about the restaurant. There's no choice for either of you.''

''I forgot all about the restaurant,'' Matt said. ''Has anyone else died? I still can't believe it was done solely to find me. Did they catch the people who did it?''

''The two men we caught who aren't covered by diplomatic immunity are being taken to Boston. They might give the police some information. Before you ask, we have a guard with your friend Dr. Farmer. He is going to fully recover. Don't feel responsible. No one in his right mind would have anticipated what happened. We aren't used to this sort of casual terrorism here in the States, but the behavior is not out of character. Remember that bar they bombed in Germany? And . . .'' Parker said slowly, watching Corey's face turn masklike, ''the buses and airplanes they routinely try to blow up. The best revenge is to finish that book and make it a best-seller.''

Parker was right. They were both in danger until Matt's book was done. That was the bottom line. She'd spend the next week or two with Matt, as she'd promised. Part of her soared with joy. There would be more memories for the cold times, but it also would make it harder to let go. So be it. She would have extra time, more cherished now that she knew in her heart that she loved him. Then, because she did love him, she'd be able to let him go.

Looking up, she realized the two men were finished talking and were staring at her in expectation, Parker with a tight, professional gaze, Matt with one open and loving. ''Did I miss something?'' she asked.

''No, not much,'' Parker told her. ''It's been decided that you and Matt will move to the condo in Mystic tonight. Hanks can stay here. You can leave a note for this Mrs. Sanders. Any other problems?''

"None that you can help me with," Corey muttered to herself as she nodded her acceptance. Not looking at either man, she rose and started down toward her office. "I'll get Matt's backup disks and show your man my alarm system. Then I'll make a list of the things that need to be done while I'm gone. You'll have to call Sean for one thing. I assume that you'll be bringing Matt's computer unless the condo already has one."

When Parker looked up at her in confusion, Corey let a slight smile cross her face. "I take it you didn't get my bill yet? It'll be there soon. It seems that some authors need more than an old typewriter."

Matt looked at Corey as she walked around her living room. Ever since they'd been back at the house, Corey had been different, distant. As soon as they were alone, he'd find out what was bothering her. He would take her in his arms and love her, hold her tight and make her share her thoughts. He'd break through whatever new barriers she'd erected. There was no way that he would lose her now.

The next hours of the afternoon passed in a blur. Parker had been on the phone incessantly, until, suddenly, everything was organized and ready. Before she had a chance to speak to Matt alone, a custom van pulled up behind her shop. Corey gave Parker a look of disbelief when she saw the lime-green creation with tropical scenes stenciled on its side. He assured her that no one would suspect it of being a government vehicle.

"You're kidding," Corey muttered as they opened the side door to deposit her two pieces of beige luggage on the green shag rug. Looking around, she saw that there was a bar, a TV, and even a small refrigerator. "And you complained when I accidentally lost that tiny Renault in Milan?"

"It's not quite the same," Parker told her soothingly. "This vehicle did not cost us a penny. It was confiscated in a drug raid. It's really quite useful for some types of stakeouts."

"Sure!" Corey agreed. "No one would *ever* notice this parked out in front of their house."

"No, not in some neighborhoods."

"Do you know what this type of van was called while I was in undergraduate school?" Matt asked, wanting to break though the cool reserve that Corey had retreated into that afternoon. Before she could answer, he told her. "Meat wagons."

"Tacky, Matt, really tacky. I suppose you had one, right?"

"No, but I always wanted to try one out." Suddenly serious, he said, "I never thought it would be under circumstances like these." Leaning over, he quietly added in a teasing voice, "We've had all kinds of firsts together."

"All right, folks," Parker ordered, "into the van, or whatever you want to call it. Corey, look at it this way . . . no one would ever suspect that anyone remotely connected to the government was traveling in it."

"You got a point, Parker," Corey admitted. Sticking her hand out, she shook Parker's hand and said, "Thanks for everything. If I don't see you again, it's been nice working for you."

Holding Corey's hand in his larger one, Parker looked into her blue eyes. "Don't write me off just yet. We'll be seeing each other again. You can bet on it."

She and Matt climbed inside the van and settled themselves on a seat that seemed more suited to a living room than a moving vehicle. Two of Parker's men rode in the front, one driving, the other watching for tails. Another car with three men followed them at a safe distance, using two-way radios as a means of communication. No one was sure if the terrorists had managed to trace Corey's license plate and they proceeded on the assumption that they were being followed.

Corey and Matt looked at each other as the car started up, their hands joining in a spontaneous gesture. Gazing through the filtered light of the van, she was mesmerized by his face, her finger reaching out to trace the line of his nose, the sharp angle of his cheekbone, the masculine curve of his jaw.

He was safe. The overwhelming relief surging through her made her nearly giddy. Above all, she wanted to throw herself into his arms, hold him tight, for now and forever. But that was not possible. She would have to make it through their last days without giving in to those impulses.

It was bad enough that she knew she loved him, heart and soul. There was no need for him to find out. He didn't need another burden, another guilt to face when he left her. Nor did he need any fuel for his fantasy that he cared for her. No nurse let her patient know she fell in love with him. Any decent psychiatrist didn't take advantage of his patients' innocent transference. Good agents didn't mistake the affection, relief, and dependence that a subject felt for love. If only she could find the strength to be a good agent this final time. Sighing, she laid her head back on the seat, exhausted from the mental as well as emotional upheaval of the day.

They finally stopped for food at a drive-through window of a fast-food restaurant. When Corey looked up to order, Matt asked her if she was all right.

"When you're holding me, everything is all right," Corey answered truthfully. "How about you? Does your head still ache?"

"Not much. I'll take a couple of aspirins tonight and be fine in the morning. Are you really all right when I hold you?"

Before Corey could answer, the truck edged forward and reached the window where the driver paid for their food. The next few minutes were spent eating, the only sound being the papers rustling, the only smell that unmistakable odor of fast food.

As soon as he finished eating, the driver started the car and they were moving again. Sipping her coffee, Corey reached over to touch the black curl that had drifted down onto Matt's forehead. "What's your home like?" she asked, wanting to know how he normally lived.

"It's a town house. Modern, three bedrooms, a fireplace. A hot tub in the backyard. I have a house-keeper who comes in three days a week, does all the cleaning, cooks my food, and freezes the rest. Is that what you want to know?"

"Tell me all about your life back in California, Matt, everything," Corey asked, trying to imagine Matt walking around in the sun, teaching classes to young people, doing whatever professors do. "Are you happy teaching?"

Matt reached over, holding Corey tightly to him. He told her about his home, and his office. He described the courses he taught and the graduate students he was working with. Piece by piece, he drew a verbal picture of his life, its good points and its bad, his colleagues, his friends, and even his enemies. He told her what kind of car he drove, and where he shopped for clothes. Softly, intimately,

Matt shared his life with Corey as they drove through the dark night, sensing in her a need to know more of him, and wanting to give her anything that she needed.

Finally, he grew silent, not knowing what else to say.

"Thank you," Corey whispered to him. "I needed to know how you live your real life."

Holding her more tightly, he reached down to kiss her hair and then her forehead, nose, and lips. "Someday I'll show you in person."

Finally, the driver of the van leaned back and told them they'd arrived in Mystic. They could smell the salt-sea air and knew that the ocean was nearby, although the combination of the dark and the New England fog made visibility very poor. "I'm going to pull into the garage," the driver instructed. "Wait until we close the door to get out."

"How far is Mystic from the Cape, anyway?" Matt asked Corey. "We've been driving for a long time. Just how far did we drive to make sure there's no one following us?"

"It's less than a hundred miles from Hamstead to Mystic, if you drive straight through. But we both know no self-respecting spy ever drives straight through. It's against the rules."

As the van stopped, Corey added, "I hope this place is as nice as Parker promised. We're going to be seeing a lot of it in the next two weeks."

Another man, a thin blond man in his midthirties, opened a door in the garage and greeted them. "Corey, sweetheart, how are you?" he asked as he reached out to give Corey a quick hug and a not-so-brief kiss. "I haven't seen you in three, four years. Parker never told me that you'd be part of this assignment. What fantastic luck!"

Turning, while still maintaining his hold on Corey's

hand, the sharp-featured Texan drawled, "Is this the dude we're supposed to be protecting?" Without a pause to wait for his answer, he stuck out his hand and introduced himself. "I'm Mike Whibney, the agent assigned to guard you while you're here."

Matt stuck out his hand. "Nice to meet you," he managed to say. Who was this guy? And just how cozy was he with Corey? Before he had a chance to do more than give Corey a searing look, Kelly and Hanks had unloaded their luggage and the computer. The two men rapidly carried their belongings up the stairs. As soon as Kelly and Hanks were back in the garage, they motioned Corey and Matt toward the open door leading to the stairway that led up from the garage to the living area. As soon as they were hidden from the street, the van backed out of the garage.

Walking up the narrow stairs, Matt felt disoriented. It seemed impossible that just twenty-four hours ago he and Corey were lying in her warm bed. Gone . . . it was all gone. He felt a desperate need to bring some of it back, to lay claim to Corey.

"Mike, it's so good to see you," Corey was exclaiming as she entered the large room at the top of the stairs. "I had no idea that you would be here."

"I'm recuperating, actually, from a nasty little bullet that I caught a month ago in Algeria. Parker called me this morning and wondered if I felt like house guests for a couple of weeks."

Corey looked around, viewing the room in amazement. It was off-white, with exposed beams and gleaming hardwood floors. Two separate area groupings of a pit type in beige velvet looked out over the river, or so she assumed. A thick drape covered two sets of sliding glass doors that opened to a deck. Excellent reproduction Queen Anne furniture filled the room. It looked not only extremely expensive but very elegant. "Some place," she said, looking around.

"It's an upscale vacation condo. There are thirty units, all on the riverfront," Michael explained. "The population is very transient and the townies pay the people who live here very little mind, sort of a reverse snobbery. The security's good, too, because of the exclusivity of the residents."

Turning around, he added, "It's a good spot. No one notices an extra guard or two, or an extra servant for that matter. The only open spot is the river, and since no one knows you're here, it shouldn't be any problem." Acknowledging Matt for the first time, he ordered, "No calls, prof."

"I learned my lesson," Matt said, resenting the other man's condescending attitude. It was painfully obvious that this conceited blond cowboy knew all the details of his stupidity.

"It was all my fault," Corey interrupted. "I should have kept a closer eye on him."

"It probably wouldn't have made any difference. If this gent didn't follow orders, you're not to blame. They must want him pretty bad to do something that desperate here in the States. It was a big operation to find one guy." Clapping Matt on the shoulder, Mike told Matt that he hoped he'd be comfortable here, and asked if they were ready to see their rooms. "You two have had quite a day. You're lucky Corey rescued you before the head honcho showed up. You might not be in such good shape right now if she hadn't."

Matt counted to ten before he began to follow Whibney and Corey up the stairs. Corey walked in the middle, and he brought up the rear. He found himself holding his breath, wondering what Corey was going to do in the next minute. Would she demand separate bedrooms? Was this one of her old boyfriends? The cowboy was certainly interested in her, letting no chance go by to remind her that Matt was an outsider, a clumsy one no less. He didn't know what he'd do if she went to a different room. Corey cared about him. Matt knew that. But did she care enough to live with him openly? Whatever she does, Matt ordered himself, he wouldn't give up.

Corey walked up the stairs fighting with herself. Here was a chance to get away from Matt. She could insist on her own bedroom, or even pretend to be taken with Michael. Goodness knows, he'd tried to get her into bed enough times. She could pretend to flirt with him, enough to hold Matt off. But the thought of another man even touching her made her nauseated. The thought of being so totally dishonest with herself and with Matt made her remember the vow she'd made after Chuck had used her. She would never, never let herself do anything she didn't want to again, for whatever reason.

Turning back, she caught a glimpse of Matt's rigid face, and that alone decided her. His eyes were bleak. His body was stiff, and he looked like a man just barely holding on to his control. She knew that he was leaving it up to her, granting her the privacy and dignity that she needed with her colleague. There was no choice. There never had been. She could no more give up her last few days with Matt than could a starving man turn down his last meal.

When Michael opened the door to a large bedroom, and started toward the next one down the hall, Corey gently stopped him. "We're together," she told the Texan firmly, ignoring the glint of surprised anger in his green eyes.

"Together?" Mike questioned, his eyes narrowing. "You've changed, little Corey, since I saw you last. Quite a bit."

"Perhaps I have," Corey told him, "but it's hardly any of your business, is it?"

"Hands off, I suppose, just like the good old days?" Michael taunted. "What's this Yank got that I don't?"

"Me," Corey said firmly. Closing the door gently, she said, "Till tomorrow, Mike. Nice seeing you again."

Corey stood for a moment, her head leaning against the wooden door. She clearly had committed herself to Matt. Now she was strangely reluctant to turn around and face him. Taking a deep breath, she tried to calm her pulse and to appear casual about the declaration she'd just made.

This isn't any big deal, she thought. She didn't know why she felt so exposed. Declaring that she and Matt were together somehow seemed to be more of a commitment than she'd planned on making, but there had been no choice. She couldn't let Matt suffer, when the truth was that she wanted to be with him, as much if not more than he wanted to be with her.

Plastering a smile on her face, Corey turned to Matt, only to hear him say three words that tore her world apart.

"I love you," he stated, eyes glowing and arms open. "I love you so very much, Corey Hamilton."

As though on a string, she was pulled to him, letting herself be enveloped in his arms, feeling warm and safe and cherished. "You don't play fair, Matt," she whispered into his broad chest, rubbing her head against his warm, muscular physique, wanting nothing more than to freeze that moment in time. "How can I resist you?"

"You can't. Admit that you can't. I know that words aren't easy for you and that I'm not what you wanted for your life," Matt whispered into the top of her blond curls, "but I love you and I swear that we can make it together."

Although Corey didn't respond verbally, she'd tightened her hold around his waist, clinging to him as though there were no tomorrow. Matt's control snapped and he reached down to claim her lips. He would make her believe, he swore to himself. He would brand himself on her body so that she would never question that she belonged to him, with him, for the rest of her life. No other man would ever hold her, touch her, or taste her sweetness but him. He would see to that, tonight, now.

Madness touched Corey as Matt's strong hands began to outline her body. His lips and tongue teased the edge of her mouth, until she opened her lips to his, seeking the spicy masculine taste that was his alone. Shifting her head, she shaped her mouth to his, unable to resist.

Tasting, caressing, his lips left Corey's hungry mouth and moved quickly down her neck, settling in the hollow at its base, finding her pulse point with his warm tongue. As he nuzzled her neck, he began to unbutton her blouse slowly and her clothing dropped away, unnoticed.

Pushing aside the spread on the queen-size bed with an impatient hand, he settled her on the sheets. He stood for a moment to look down at his woman, at her passion-drugged surrender. Smoky eyes, eyes so dilated that they appeared black, smoldered up at him. Her body gleamed in the soft light of the lamp.

His gleaming blue eyes lingered where his hands itched to be, feasting first on the pointed breasts that awaited his mouth, then following the line of her long, slim torso with its faintly rounded hips, to linger on the second thatch of golden curls, concealing all the secrets he knew and cherished.

Corey's eyes didn't leave his for a second as he slowly stripped off his clothes. She watched him looking at her, feeling as though his gaze were the warm sun, its heat flowing all over her body. She reached for Matt's hand and slowly, slowly pulled him down to her.

He moved to her side, but not fully on top of her as she'd urged. *Tonight has just begun*, Matt thought as he reached out one long finger and drew a line from Corey's lush mouth down her chin, down her pulsing neck and between her breasts. Pausing for a moment, he traced a lazy trail over each mound and back again, before continuing in his journey down her warm, sensitive body.

His finger teased first one hip then the other as it worked its way around and over and finally into her navel. Then lower still, Matt's finger traced, making patterns on first one satin smooth thigh, then the other. As Corey moaned, Matt pushed her legs slightly apart and retraced his circular patterns of fire on her inner thighs, slowly approaching her throbbing center, only to retreat again and again.

When Corey tried to pull him to her, he turned her over onto her stomach and began his journey back, this time tracing his path with his tongue. Slowly, he laved the back of her legs and spent precious minutes cherishing the tender skin behind her knees before he moved further, up, beyond the perfect backside to find her spine, where he kissed each and every tiny indentation.

As Corey lay beside him, facedown in the pillow, biting the material to control her moans, trembling with need, Matt moved up to his knees. He positioned himself within her outspread legs, then reaching around her body, grabbing her tender-swollen breasts with his hands as he entered her swiftly. Corey shook with surprised passion as his mouth assaulted her neck and shoulders with tender, biting kisses while his hands, his clever fingers, first circled and then moved over the diamond-hard nipples that throbbed in his hands.

He moved within her, slowly at first as her body adjusted to the unusual position, then more rapidly as she sought his rhythm. With stunning rapidity, Matt moved his left arm from her breast and used it to totally cover her chest, pressing his forearm against both of her throbbing nipples. He used his other hand, now free, to move under her body and enter the golden delta of her femininity and to seek the center of her being. Corey went crazy in his arms as her body burst forth into a glorious conclusion, shuddering again and again first against Matt's hand and then against his hardness that anchored her, firmly caught in his sensual trap.

Corey lay quietly, still imprisoned between Matt and the silky sheets, when he softly withdrew from her body, causing Corey to twist over her shoulder and plant a passionate kiss on his mouth. When she began to question him, "Matt . . . why didn't you?" wondering why he had not joined her in the wonder and glory that she felt, Matt whispered words of praise into her mouth and told her, "Love, this is but the beginning."

As Corey lay on her stomach, golden sensations flowing down her body, she felt Matt's warm tongue begin to lave her back, slowly licking and nibbling over first one warm shoulder and then the other. Lower, lower he went, kissing first one side of her body and then the other. When he reached her waist, Corey began to stir in his arms, murmuring incoherent questions into her pillow, her hands making futile gestures in her attempt to touch him.

"Soon, my love, soon," he whispered, soothing her questing lips with a touch of his finger. He rubbed her swollen lips with his thumb, groaning when she took it into her mouth and ran her tongue over it.

"Please, Matt, I want you, too. Let me touch you, too."

Taking her hand into his, he kissed its palm tenderly and turned it over to caress each knuckle. Slowly he worked his way up her arm, to her elbow, where he ran his tongue back and forth across the crease and showed Corey that there were places on her body that no man had ever caressed before.

Still he worshiped, still he desired, still he cherished her. Dipping his head toward her femininity once again, he drove her near, almost over the edge of passion, and then retreated. When he returned, taking her with a frantic passion, he drove her high and higher until she shuddered in his strong arms. Then he began again, showing Corey that she was capable of more passion than she'd thought existed within the world.

Moment by moment, she fell deeper beneath his spell—and by the time that his bold mouth once again reached her lips, she turned to him with blinding passion. Gripping her hands into his hair, she pulled him to her, murmuring words of love into his mouth, finally unable to hold back her innermost thought. "Come to me, come to me."

"I love you, Corey," Matt whispered as he finally allowed his body to ease over hers. Propped on his knees, he found his way between her legs, and Corey immediately caught his body with her long limbs. Urgently, she locked her knees and pulled him, her feminine softness needing, craving the release that only he could bring to her.

When Matt finally moved into Corey with a silken thrust that left her breathless, she gasped and pulled him to her. "I love you, Matt, I love you," she confessed as he began to move within her, with her, and for her. Faster and faster, harder and harder, they moved into ecstasy. They were joined in a moment of pure passion and pure love, perfect, timeless and forever binding.

Tired beyond words and content beyond belief, they fell asleep. Matt awoke a few hours later and turned off the light, surprised to find that it was still dark. He pulled a cover over Corey and watched her in the gentle light that prefaces the day's harsher glare of reality. He walked to the window and stood, his arms clasped behind him, wondering what would happen next. He'd never felt like this before, never been so out of control. Never had he branded a woman as his own property. The only thing that gave him hope were the words that he'd forced from her, the truth that she did love him. That and the knowledge that if she truly had wanted him to stop, he would have.

Corey awoke, feeling somehow bereft. She saw Matt wander to the window and bow his head in thought. His stance bespoke a troubled mind. Last night had changed something in Corey and she lay for a moment, wondering what it was. She felt both more and less free. She knew that she had never been loved like that before and never could be again, for some elemental part of her had passed to him and from that day forward a part of her belonged to Matt—whenever he wanted her, wherever she was. Silently she walked to him, and with a slight touch of her hand, reached to feel his brow.

"I didn't mean to wake you," Matt told her, his eyes searching for hers in the gloom. "Are you . . . all right?"

"I'm fine. Why shouldn't I be?"

Reaching for her, and pulling her firmly into his arms, Matt whispered into her ear, "I'm sorry for being so . . . so . . . forceful. I love you, need you so." Looking at the river sparkling in the moonlight distance, he told her, "I was jealous of that Texan and ashamed of how I'd botched up by calling the hospital. Damn it, I was frightened of losing you. It's not much of an excuse, but it's the truth."

"You don't need an excuse. You did nothing that I didn't want—nothing. You could never hurt me, never do anything to make me want you less. Come back to bed, we can talk in the morning."

"You really love me?" Matt asked as they walked back to the bed. When she nodded her head, Matt gathered her into his arms and showed her another side of his love—a gentle, sweet side.

THIRTEEN

"Corey! Corey!" Matt shouted exuberantly as he unlocked the door to their suite at the hotel and dropped his briefcase on a table. The suite consisted of a formal living room and separate bedroom, complete with queen-size bed, that overlooked Central Park. The luxurious accommodations were first class all the way, from the brocade wallpaper and formal furniture to the fully stocked refrigerator and liquor cabinet.

Parker had made certain that a great deal of publicity surrounded Matt's arrival in New York and the official acceptance of his manuscript by a prestigious publisher. He'd been interviewed, taped, recorded, even appeared on live television. Matt had come out of hiding in a big way, and was no longer in danger.

"I'm done for the day. The book will be out in two months and best of all . . ." Matt paused, after he looked up and realized that no one was there. He called her name again as he walked into the bedroom, and then peeked into the bathroom. For a moment he let himself hope that he'd find her chin-deep in bubbles, and that they would reenact a particularly erotic evening they'd spent in the oversize tub.

Instead of a bubbling tub, Matt found an empty room, too empty. Even Corey's toothbrush was missing. The only personal items remaining were his own.

Rushing now, he threw open the closet of the bedroom and realized all her clothing was gone. "Damn it all." He should have suspected something like this. It had been this very afternoon that Parker had given him the final all clear. It was also the first time that Corey had left his side. She was supposed to be shopping for their trip to California. But she hadn't gone shopping, she'd just gone.

Sitting down on the bed, unable to absorb the fact that she'd left without even a good-bye, he noticed the letter lying on the table by his side of the bed. Picking it up with trembling fingers, he held it for a moment, knowing it was a farewell letter, hoping against hope that it was not. He read:

My dearest Matt,

Forgive me for leaving like this. Parker will tell you today that you are safe and can return to your own life. The movie's over.
Be happy.

The note was unsigned, as though Corey could not bear to write her name, finalize her good-bye. What had gone wrong? Why hadn't he seen that she would run? Why hadn't he noticed that she had never outright agreed with him, never actually said yes to all of his plans in all of their time together?

They'd awakened the first morning in Mystic still warm with each other's love, still tangled within their magic. Mike had knocked at their door, threatening to come in unless they dragged themselves out of bed, making Corey blush when she realizd that he must have heard the muffled cries of love they'd made when they first woke up.

Once Michael realized that Corey was fully committed to Matt, he forgot his jealousy. Their days settled down into a routine. Matt worked while Corey and Michael found various ways to pass the time. Corey spent several hours reading and editing Matt's book, adding several small illustrative incidents and giving him encouragement as she watched it all come together. She was amazed at what Matt had found out, as well as dumbfounded by the duplicity that he'd uncovered. His accounting background had allowed him to follow the money, and the trail was indeed an interesting and incriminating one.

In time, Matt actually began to like Mike, seeing his easy charm and ready wit. So much so, that one night Matt'd asked Corey how she'd been able to resist him.

"I never had any trouble resisting anyone until you came along. You flat out threw me for a loop, Matthew Stone," Corey had told him honestly. "I've never felt this way before."

They'd loved fully and wondrously that night and Matt had started to feel a real confidence in his relationship with Corey. Once she'd spoken of leaving him, only once. It was late night and they'd stepped to the third-story balcony off their bedroom. The moon was full and reflected off the river that moved in front of their window. The tide was going out that night and the water rushed under the drawbridge, past the warf, and out to the sea.

The tang of the saltwater and the lonely wail of a

fog horn had put them both in a pensive mood. Matt had held Corey close, to warm her and reassure himself. "I'll miss this place," Corey'd whispered into the night.

"We'll come back," Matt promised. "When this is over, we'll explore the whole town, see the other side of the bridge. Maybe we'll rent a boat and go out to the sea for the day."

"If only we could," she whispered into his chest. "If only we could. If only the story wouldn't end."

When Matt looked at her, she held him tight and let him comfort her in the age-old manner. As her eyes glazed with passion, Matt heard her whisper, "I love you, Matt. I really love you. Enough to want only the best for you."

When he told her that she was his wish, that she was the best, she smiled and showed him a soft, desperate love that he had never known before. That night she had been the aggressor, forcing him to lie on the bed, his arms over his head, as she'd made him wait for her love.

She led him back from the moonlit balcony and pushed him down on the bed, kneeling by his side. Her soft tongue and tender lips feasted on his neck, his chest, and his firm stomach. She feverishly explored his navel, the soft skin on the inside of his thighs, and ultimately his satiny hardness, teasing and testing his strength with both tongue and teeth. Like the wind, she moved over him until he begged for her to ease the ache, to complete the other half of his being. Finally, she'd settled over him and took him into her slowly, one inch at a time, until he was trembling with need and restraint.

More than anything, he wanted to grab her hips and forge a pathway to her center. More than anything, he wanted the glorious torture to continue. When she settled over him, taking all of of him that there was to take, she'd reached down to kiss his lips and move his hands to her throbbing breasts.

Madness and moonlight intertwined, and they flew together, rode together, out over the sea and onto a wave that crested, higher and higher until they were not sure which body was his and which hers, which mouth groaned and which murmured of love and need. That night, there was no difference between them.

Now she was gone, and Matt felt some vital part of him went with her. He reread the letter, as if he thought the words would change and he could make some sense out of what she wrote. What the hell did she mean, the movie's over? he wondered. Suddenly a memory returned, to one of the early days they shared, before the kidnapping and move to Mystic. He had made some dumb remark about their existence seeming like a James Bond movie. She'd said something even then, about it paralleling their existence, but he'd not taken her seriously. Could she possibly think that he was that shallow, that stupid? That he didn't know that he loved her, needed her?

Anger built, and determination. Matt stood up. No way was he going to lose her now, not after what they'd gone through together. Not when he knew that she loved him, loved him enough to let him go. "Well," Matt proclaimed out loud, "I'm not so blasted noble. I'm not about to let her go, no matter what."

Striding to the phone, he demanded an outside line and punched Parker's number. When the efficient secretary finally connected Matt to Parker, Matt cut him off in the middle of his greeting. "I want to know where Corey is," he demanded.

"How would I know? She doesn't work for me anymore, Stone. Remember? As far as I know, she's with you. Has she gotten lost?"

"Can it, Parker. Tell me, is she in any danger? Now that you've said I was all right, I assume that she is, too."

"Far as I know, Matt. If she's gone, it is because she wants to be."

"Would you tell me if she came back to work for you?"

"I don't think you have to worry about that." After a pause, Parker asked, "What are you going to do?"

"Find her, what else can I do?"

"You could let her go, now that you don't need her protection anymore," the older man in Washington suggested.

"No way. Look, thanks for your help, I'll—"

It was Parker's turn to interrupt, and he did before Matt could hang up. "Remember, she's had a hard time and she acts a lot tougher than she is. For what it's worth, I think she loves you. Don't go after her unless you're very sure," Parker told the younger man slowly. "Call me if you need any help."

"Thanks," Matt murmured in a surprised voice. Who would have thought that the bureaucrat would turn out to be human after all? Parker did care about Corey. It was as unmistakable as it was surprising. For once, he was not thinking about the agency.

If she hadn't gone back to Washington, she must have returned to her shop, Matt decided. A plan in mind, he called the front desk and arranged to have a rented car delivered to the front of the hotel and a bellhop to come up for his bags. He called his agent and canceled the rest of his appearances, telling the startled man that he'd be in touch when he was done honeymooning.

That was his intent as he drove up the Cape. That was the goal he had in mind as he finally turned down the small street on Cape Cod. Not until he turned down her street and saw the Antique Emporium sign swinging in the wind did he begin to worry. The closed sign in the window was like a slap in the face. It was only four o'clock and Matt had been sure that she'd be there, in her shop, catching up on her paperwork. He walked slowly around to the back, further losing heart when he saw no lights, only a note to the paperboy, telling him to discontinue the paper until she contacted him. Her car was gone and the entire yard had a look of desolation about it.

Matt sat on the back porch, his knees up and his face resting in his hands. He could wait here until she came back, he decided, for sooner or later, she had to come back. He didn't dare try to break into the place; he knew that Corey would have left all the alarms turned on. He thought of questioning her neighbors, looking up her friend Sean McCaulley. How many retirement homes could there be on Cape Cod? As he stood up, ready to start his quest, he thought of the right place to look. The Sanders' house.

He was right. He knew it the minute he pulled up the driveway. Her car was down far in back and not visible from the road, but it was there. If she wouldn't answer the door, he would break in. No way would she be able to escape him!

He walked up to the wraparound porch and opened

the screen door. "Corey!" he shouted as he rattled the back door. "I know you're in there and if you don't open up, I'm going to break in." He paused and waited for a minute, wondering if she would let him in or not. When he heard nothing, he shouted again, rattling the door, this time pounding on it as well.

"All right, lady." he mumbled to himself as he eased out of his gray suit jacket. "If you want it the hard way, you'll get it the hard way." He walked to the window next to the door and wrapped his hand in the jacket when he heard a slight movement in the room. "Corey, let me in this minute or the window is gone."

Corey stood on the widow's walk, her face to the wind, in the gathering dusk when she heard his car pull up. A sense of inevitability came over her as she walked down the stairs. Part of her hoped that he would come after her, but nothing would change. It would only make it harder for them both. She was a coward that morning when she left the note, but she didn't want to face him, didn't want to deal with this final confrontation.

Why couldn't he let things end; why did he have to make this so bloody difficult for them both? Now she would have to tell him everything. Then watch him walk away when he found the truth. She was not good enough for him, not pure and good and untouched like his beloved Sally.

Matt had been so wonderful once they had arrived in New York. The day he turned his manuscript in, it seemed as though a black cloud had lifted from his shoulders. He was the same man, just happier, freer, younger. Worst of all, Corey found she loved him all the more, and, for a few stolen days, she'd enjoyed herself with a freedom that was as foreign to her as it was precious. Between interviews they played and laughed like teenagers, and wined and dined like sophisticated yuppies. They had seen two Broadway shows and even made a brief stop at one of New York's jazzy nightspots. They had walked and talked and been so happy that Corey thought she might burst.

Now she was hoping that she could manage to get through these next few minutes without making a fool of herself. Silently she opened the door, hearing Matt sigh in relief. He was relieved that she wasn't going to hide anymore. He had half expected to literally chase her down and tackle her before she'd let him have a chance to talk.

Not that she looked very encouraging as he walked into the room and looked at her. She'd been crying. Her eyes were red and swollen, her face blotchy. Turning her back to him, she asked in a cool tone, reminiscent of their first meeting, "What do you want?"

Fighting back his impulse for a fast retort, Matt walked to her and placed his hands on either side of her face. Before she could struggle free, he gave his answer. "You. I want you. For now and forever."

"Don't say that," Corey pleaded, closing her eyes, cursing herself when she felt a tear trickle down her cheek against her will. "I'm no good for you, Matt. I told you in my note to let it go. We had a wonderful affair. Now it's over."

"No way, lady, is it over. I don't know what you thought it was, but for me it wasn't any affair—it was love, the real, forever-after kind, and I'm not letting you go."

"It was just the situation, like a patient falling for his nurse. Nothing more."

"Like hell, Corey. This is the second time in my life that I've really been in love, and I know the difference between this and some momentary affair. I've had my share of those and there is a big difference."

"It won't work, Matt," Corey denied, pulling from his hold and walking into the living room. She walked over to a blue Victorian sofa and sat down. "You need a whole woman to love, one whom you can build a life with."

"Right, and that woman is you. We're going to get married and have ten kids and live happily ever after," Matt insisted, coming to kneel before her on the floor. "Marry me, Corey—and share my life," he pleaded. "I've never loved anyone as I love you."

"You don't know me, you don't know what I've done," Corey argued, telling herself not to give in to him, not to do what she wanted to more than anything else. "Remember the day on Cape Cod. I had a gun in my hand. I was choking that man. I knocked him out. If I'd had to, I would have killed him."

"So what? I would have killed him to protect you, my love. I will do anything to protect you, now or in the future. There's nothing you could have done that could change the way I feel about you. Nothing. I know you've been an agent. I imagine you've seen things that are terrible, maybe even done things that you didn't approve of. I love the woman you are today, and that includes your past. All of it."

When she started to talk, Matt put tender fingers up to her lips. "Let me go on," he said. "I know you better than you know yourself. You would never do anything that I would not understand, nothing that I could not forgive. You are the most moral person I've ever met, and I know that whatever you did, it was done out of patriotism and loyalty to our government."

"Moral!" Corey laughed. "You think I'm so moral? So wonderful and patriotic. Do you think being wrapped in the flag always makes it right? Do you tell the veterans from Vietnam not to have nightmares because they did it all for the right reasons?"

"Love, the nightmare might not go away, but the guilt has to stop. Their reasons were right; so were yours. No one started out with anything but the best of intentions."

"You helped me to see that it wasn't my fault that Sally and my son died. Can't I help you see that you can forgive yourself for whatever sins you imagine?"

When Corey only shook her head, Matt went on. Softly, he told her one truth that she found difficult, if not, impossible to deny. "Ask yourself this . . ." Matt insisted, locking his eyes with hers. "If it were me in this situation, if it were all reversed. If I had done the identical things that are haunting you, would it make any difference in your love for me? Do you think so little of me that you believe I'm not allowed to love as deeply as you are?"

Tears falling, Corey permitted herself to fall into his arms. She could resist his tenderness no longer, fight against his understanding no more. Brokenly, she told him about Chuck and her reasons for leaving the agency. She recounted those painful last days, the innocent people dead, the situation so much like the one that killed his wife that she dared him to forgive her.

After she finished, she lay in his arms, waiting for him to withdraw, passive now, too spent to wonder why he'd taken so long to speak. With love in his eyes, he stroked her hair. "I remember the incident,

Corey. It happened just before I decided to write my book. I can see how you think you're responsible for all those deaths, but you aren't. The people who do things like that are crazy, and the crazy things they do aren't our fault. You did your duty, love. Even if Chuck had reported it, if you'd gone over his head to report it yourself, what's to prove the results would have been different? Once those terrorists decided to hijack a bus, it was out of your hands. If it hadn't been that particular bus, it would have been the next. If they'd been taken into custody for questioning, other zealots would have taken their places and they would have had one more excuse for the next atrocity.

"Don't you see that we can't control the world?" Matt asked her, shaking her gently. "Neither one of us can. Using your logic, aren't I to blame for the ten people injured in Boston? If I weren't writing my book, those people would not have been hurt. The only ones to blame are those who did it. Not us, not the innocent bystanders, not the people who are trying to help. Only them." Turning her to look at him, he tenderly kissed her. "No more guilt. It was not your fault. Period. Now, let's talk about us and our ten children. When can we get started?"

"Wait a minute, Stone. What is this ten children bit?" Corey demanded. "I never agreed to have ten children. That's crazy!"

"Okay, how many do you want?"

"Four, tops," Corey responded before she could stop herself, catching the twinkle in Matt's eyes. Laughing, she collapsed in his arms once more, torn between tears of joy and those of anguish. "You won't give up, will you? You tricked me, didn't you, with the ten children?"

"Right again. It's all in the way you phrase the

question. Once we decided on children, the number really didn't matter. It's all negotiable after that. We political science teachers are best when negotiating. Didn't I ever tell you that I teach a course on the fine art of treaties and international courts?''

''Not that I recall. Do you really?''

''No, but it sounds good, doesn't it.'' Suddenly serious, Matt stood up and pulled her to him, groaning that he was getting too old to stay on his knees anymore. ''Please marry me. I love you with all my heart and I'll do my best to make you happy.''

Unable to fight anymore, unwilling to run any farther, Corey nodded her head in agreement. ''I love you, Matt, more than I ever thought possible.''

''No more hiding, for either of us,'' Matt rasped as he took her into his arms, into his heart, and forever into his life.

The old house on the point glistened in the darkness. Christmas lights were strung over the porch and candles flickered in each and every window. The lights reflected off the water, making the eyes blink, for a moment, in confusion. The pinecone wreaths on the front and back doors added to the spell as did the light coating of snow that dusted the roof.

Inside the house, two people sat on the floor in front of a fire, holding antique crystal glasses of a sparkling purple liquid. A large Christmas tree twinkled in the corner, presents already cascading from under its branches even though Christmas Day was still eight days away. ''Next year, my love, it will be champagne,'' the man promised his wife. She agreed, although amiably noting that the grape juice was almost as tasty, and certainly more economical.

Matt reached over to caress Corey's swollen stomach and agreed. "Nothing could be better than this, my love. Except, next Christmas, when we will be three."

Seriously, Corey turned to him and asked a question that she often thought, yet had hesitated to ask him. "We never talked much about your son. Does my being pregnant bring back too many memories?"

Leaning back, Matt put his head on what remained of Corey's lap. "No, not really. That was another life. I'll always love Tommy and keep a part of him in my heart. As I have Sally. I don't know how to say this, exactly, but I cherish his memory and am grateful that I was privileged enough to love him and be loved by him, even if it was for all too brief a time."

Turning, he placed a series of small kisses on Corey's moving stomach, pulling up her maternity top and down her loose jeans to place his ear against her flesh. "I love you and the child we've made. I've never been as happy, or content as now."

"I'm glad, so glad," Corey whispered. She'd always worried a bit, about all the many changes Matt had made to accommodate his life with hers. He was now teaching at Harvard with his friend Harry, and they lived most of the year in Massachusetts. With the royalties from his book, Matt had purchased the old house that Corey loved as a wedding gift for her. They came to the Cape every summer and semester break, as well as occasional weekends. She'd kept her antique shop, a young couple managing it as well as occupying the top apartment, while she did the buying. Their lives had blended very happily together. And now, in four months, they would have their first child.

"Matt," Corey protested as she felt his fingers

tugging at her slacks. "Stop that. We're expecting Parker to arrive any minute from Washington for the weekend." After Corey had left the agency for good, they'd found Parker still interested in their lives. As a friend. In fact, he'd appointed himself honorary godfather to their first child.

"He called a few minutes ago, when you were getting the drinks, and said he'll be delayed for at least three hours."

"Why didn't you tell me?" Corey asked, allowing herself to lean back onto the soft cushions that were piled by the fire.

"I'm telling you now," he informed her as his other hand inched its way up her blouse and began to unbutton its front.

"What are you doing?" Corey squealed in mock protest as she moved to lie down next to her husband and unbutton his shirt.

"Showing you how much I love you," he rasped as he placed a tender kiss on her growing tummy. "Showing you how much I want you now, and forever."

With great joy, Corey proceeded to show him the very same thing.